"I can't marry you,"
Misty said with a gasp.

From Luc's expression she could tell he felt affronted. "I won't accept that," he said firmly. "I fulfilled all your specifications."

"We aren't in love."

He shrugged. "Define *love* for me. I know I want to marry you. I know you told me you wanted no other type of relationship. So I'm all set."

"This is crazy," Misty whispered to herself.

"I'll make you happy," he promised.

"You'll hate me in three months," she vowed.

"Never." He stared down at her with an expression that set off a throbbing pulse in her very core...

Dear Reader:

Romance readers today have more choice among books than ever before. But with so many titles to choose from, deciding what to select becomes increasingly difficult.

At SECOND CHANCE AT LOVE we try to make that decision easy for you — by publishing romances of the highest quality every month. You can confidently buy any SECOND CHANCE AT LOVE romance and know it will provide you with solid romantic entertainment.

Sometimes you buy romances by authors whose work you've previously read and enjoyed — which makes a lot of sense. You're being sensible . . . and careful . . . to look for satisfaction where you've found it before.

But if you're *too* careful, you risk overlooking exceptional romances by writers whose names you don't immediately recognize. These first-time authors may be the stars of tomorrow, and you won't want to miss any of their books! At SECOND CHANCE AT LOVE, many writers who were once "new" are now the most popular contributors to the line. So trying a new writer at SECOND CHANCE AT LOVE isn't really a risk at all. Every book we publish must meet our rigorous standards — whether it's by a popular "regular" or a newcomer.

In the months to come, we urge you to watch for these names — Linda Raye, Karen Keast, Betsy Osborne, Dana Daniels, and Cinda Richards. All are dazzling new writers, an elite few whose books are destined to become "keepers." We think you'll be delighted and excited by their first books with us!

Look, too, for romances by writers with whom you're already warmly familiar: Jeanne Grant, Ann Cristy, Linda Barlow, Elissa Curry, Jan Mathews, and Liz Grady, among many others.

Best wishes,

Ellen Edwards

Ellen Edwards, Senior Editor
SECOND CHANCE AT LOVE
The Berkley Publishing Group
200 Madison Avenue
New York, N.Y. 10016

MYSTIQUE

ANN CRISTY

**SECOND CHANCE AT LOVE
BOOK**

Other books by *Ann Cristy*

Second Chance at Love
FROM THE TORRID PAST   #49
TORN ASUNDER   #60
ENTHRALLED   #103
NO GENTLE POSSESSION   #166

To Have and to Hold
TREAD SOFTLY   #3
HOMECOMING   #24

MYSTIQUE

First edition published October 1984

First printing

"Second Chance at Love" and the butterfly emblem are trademarks belonging to Jove Publications, Inc.

Printed in the United States of America

Second Chance at Love books are published by
The Berkley Publishing Group
200 Madison Avenue, New York, NY 10016

*To my husband
and wonderful men everywhere
who create an aura
of love around women*

The strength, gentleness,
and giving in a relationship
create a mystique of love.

CHAPTER ONE

MISTY CARVER, KNOWN professionally as Mystique, enjoyed playing the piano in the Edwardian Room of Manhattan's Terrace Hotel, but she didn't like playing for private parties there, especially during the Christmas season. In the eight months since she'd begun working at the posh midtown hotel, she had discovered that private audiences tended to be more boisterous and undisciplined than regular guests. Tonight was the third party she had played for that week, and she was exhausted.

During her break, Willis, the maître d', told her, "The Manhattan Stuyvesant Bank always holds its employee Christmas party here. One of the directors of the bank is part owner of the hotel."

"Really?" Misty asked with mild interest, rising from the piano bench.

Willis placed a hand on her arm to stop her and spoke in a hushed voice. "Well, what do you know? The man himself is here."

Flexing her tired hands and arching her aching back, Misty followed Willis's gaze around the richly decorated room hung with maroon velvet draperies and bordered with oak wainscoting. "Who?"

"Lucas Stuyvesant Harrison, director of the Manhattan Stuyvesant Bank and part owner of this hotel . . . and half of the real estate on this island," Willis added under his breath.

"By island, do you mean Manhattan?" Misty asked. Willis nodded, and they followed Luc Harrison's tall, elegantly dressed figure as he threaded his way past tables clustered around the small dance floor. Pausing in the doorway, Misty watched the striking man stride into the opulent lobby.

As Willis turned to a newly arrived couple and asked to see their invitations, Misty took a deep breath and proceeded down the wide corridor past the powder room to the Elm Bar, where she often had a drink between sets. She had just reached the bar when a rich baritone voice coming from behind her sent a shiver up her spine. "Mystique?"

She fixed a smile on her face and turned. "I'm sorry, I'm in rather a hurry. I'm . . ." Her voice trailed off as her eyes traveled up Luc Harrison's tall, masculine form and encountered a pair of deep brown eyes.

"I know. You're taking a break. I've been waiting for a chance to speak with you. I'm Luc Harrison, and I wondered if you would join me at my table for a drink."

His hair was ash blond, almost silver. The short, tousled locks fell with a casual artistry that could have been achieved only by a master barber. His tuxedo was of dark brown silk. The pleats of his cream silk shirt had been sewn with matching brown thread. His eyes roved over her, lazy, calm, self-assured.

Anger rose unbidden in her at his slow perusal. Luc Harrison oozed arrogant male confidence. Obviously few women ever turned him down. But Misty had promised herself seven months ago never to let herself be a shadow in any man's life. No more giving herself away to greedy takers. She was her own woman now, and she liked it that way.

"Sorry. I'm on my way to the ladies' room." She flashed her most professional smile, whirled away, and strode back down the hall, nodding to staff members who greeted her and listening with half an ear to the hum of conversation coming from the nearby Terrace Restaurant.

Misty used the bathroom, washed her hands, and began to repair her makeup in front of the wide mirror. She paused after glossing her lips and stared at herself. "My, my, wasn't Mr. Harrison impressive?" she asked her mirror image, noting casually that her long red-gold hair was properly tousled and that the skintight green satin dress clung to every curve.

She never needed to wear heavy clothing when she was working. Energy and excitement bubbled through her, warming her, allowing her to lose herself in the music and forget for a time the emptiness of her life. There was no way she'd take on a man like him again, Misty told herself silently. She'd had enough of them. She was just beginning to climb out of the pit. She glanced up as another woman entered the powder room.

The woman flicked her a nervous smile. "You're Mystique, aren't you?" Misty nodded and smiled. "You play so well."

"Thank you." Misty smiled again, pleased by the compliment. It gave her a lift to know that her music, which meant so much to her, also gave enjoyment to other people. Music was her lifeline, the one thing that could chase away the shadows.

Misty left the powder room and headed back toward the Elm Bar. Suddenly she felt a hand cup her elbow. She stiffened and turned, her eyes widening at the sight of Luc Harrison. His eyes pinned her sharply. A muscle tightened in his jaw. "Mr. Harrison, if you'll excuse me," she said coolly. "I only have a few minutes."

"Of course." He released her, but his voice and eyes remained cold.

She entered the Elm Bar and went at once to a stool at the very end of the bar next to the pickup station for the cocktail waitresses. "Hi, Steve."

"Hello, Mystique. The usual?" When she nodded, Steve plunked down in front of her an icy cold glass of mineral water and lime juice.

"I'll have an Irish whisky on the rocks," said a deep voice behind her.

Without acknowledging Luc Harrison's presence, she sipped her drink and watched his silk-covered arm lift the glass of dark liquid and glistening ice. All at once, without reason, she felt a frisson of panic—as though someone had brandished a weapon under her nose. She shivered.

"Cold, darling?" The soft query shot through her, stiffening her spine.

She set the glass down on the bar, making sure it was dead center on the cocktail napkin, and swung off the stool to her feet.

"Stay. You haven't finished your drink," Luc Harrison said.

"I've had enough."

The muscle in his jaw jumped again. His mouth tightened into a thin, hard line. "As you wish."

A shudder ran through her as she wended her way past small tables crowded with people, many of whom recognized and spoke to her. Moments later, she was back at her piano in the Edwardian Room.

For the rest of the evening, as the staff of the Manhattan Stuyvesant Bank danced, drank, and laughed, Misty played the piano like an automaton, aware the whole time of Luc Harrison's cool dark eyes riveted on her.

The party began to break up at three in the morning. As Misty watched a man stagger out to the lobby, Willis leaned toward her and said, "The big boss has arranged for all his people to be sent home in taxis."

"That's a blessing." Misty tried to smile, but her face felt stiff with tension and fatigue. At least Luc Harrison hadn't made any attempt to approach her again.

Once the crowd had dispersed, she shot a quick glance around the room. Luc was gone. Relief . . . and disappointment . . . flooded through her.

Soon she was stepping out into the chill December night and inhaling the clear, frosty air. The doorman waved down a cab for her. "Thank you, Frank," she called, slipping inside.

"See you tomorrow night, Mystique."

Relaxing against the seat cushions as the cab shot forward, she sighed deeply, welcoming her weariness. Only when she was deeply tired did sleep come easily to her.

As she closed her eyes, Richard and Leonard appeared like ghosts in her thoughts. She knew she was remembering them because of her encounter with Luc Harrison that evening.

Richard Lentz had come into her life during her last year at the Eastman School of Music in Rochester. A shared love of music had drawn them together. Richard had been majoring in clarinet. She'd attended school on a piano scholarship.

At first they had talked for hours about their music, the subject uppermost in both their minds. Misty had been delighted to meet someone with the same consuming desire to excel. Music had deepened their interest in each other and formed the primary bond that tied their lives together.

During their last semester at school, when they had become inseparable companions, though not lovers, Richard had said, "I'm amazed that you don't live at home and commute to school, Misty. It would be so much cheaper."

"I just prefer to live near the school," she had said, hedging. "It's more convenient." She had hesitated to tell Richard that she was glad to be away from home, away from her parents. How could she explain that, after her happy childhood, her parents' attitude toward her had subtly but dramatically changed? She prayed she would never again feel about herself the way she had during the last few years she had lived with them.

Not until just before graduation had she told Richard that she lived with her aunt and uncle, not with her parents. "When I was sixteen I asked if I could live with Aunt Lizabeth and Uncle Charles, and they said yes."

"Didn't your parents mind?"

"No, not really. They have three other children to raise, and my aunt and uncle don't have any." Misty had smiled as she'd remembered the loving, strictly disciplined life she'd lived with her aunt and uncle before going to the Eastman School.

"Oh, I see. You did it to make them happy." Richard hadn't seemed to notice that she didn't actually agree with him. Nor had he questioned her further.

After graduation she and Richard had decided to move to New York, live together, and look for work in their chosen field. Their determination to succeed had been fired by mutual enthusiasm. They were sure that plum jobs would fall into their laps. Misty had been relieved when Richard had informed her he wasn't interested in getting married or starting a family. When she'd left her parents' home, she'd made a firm promise to herself never to have children. The fear that she might treat her own offspring as her parents had treated her gnawed constantly at her.

Misty's initiation into physical love with Richard had been a somewhat painful and disillusioning experience, but she'd hidden her feelings and told him she was content. Occasionally, she'd had the uncomfortable feeling that their relationship should be based on more than a shared interest in music, but she'd shrugged her doubts away.

Misty had found a job at a piano bar almost immediately, but Richard had held out for orchestral work and remained unemployed. Sometimes it had irked her to come home from work to find that he hadn't even made the bed or washed the breakfast dishes.

"You're just feeling superior because you have a job and I don't," he had stormed at her, his slight frame quivering with rage, his horn-rimmed glasses falling askew on his nose. "Well, let me tell you, Misty, I'll never waste my classical training by playing in a bar."

"It beats starving," Misty had shot back, furious.

Afterward, she'd spent an hour apologizing to him.

When Richard had finally landed a job, he'd helped out even less in their apartment. They'd quarreled about it.

"You never stop denigrating what I do," Misty had argued, "but you don't mind using my money to buy concert tickets for you and your friends."

"Concerts are an important part of a musician's education," Richard had retorted.

"I'm a musician. Why didn't you get a ticket for me?"

"You play piano in a bar," Richard had scoffed.

The next day Misty had found a tiny studio apartment just two blocks away and moved out. She and Richard had lived together for one year, yet she had felt only relief at their parting.

After that, Misty had dated other men, but she hadn't become seriously involved with anyone until three years later, at the age of twenty-five, when she'd met Leonard Glassman, a rising account executive with an advertising firm. After they had dated for three months, Leonard had insisted that she move in with him. He had been very caring, eager to shower her with gifts, and willing to help clean the apartment. She'd told herself she really didn't mind when he woke her up each morning to make love—even though she usually didn't get to bed until three or four in the morning. "For God's sake, Misty, I thought we cared about each other," he'd exclaimed. "Isn't that why we live together?"

"Yes, but caring goes both ways," she'd answered. "We have to be considerate of each other."

"You have a great place to live, I give you money for your clothes . . ."

"I don't spend your money. I have my own," she'd muttered as she'd let him make love to her exhausted body.

Leonard had also wanted her to meet his co-workers and entertain them at home occasionally. Although she'd done her best, she'd begun to chafe at his constant demands.

"Lord, why are you always so tired?" he'd complained.

Misty had felt confused and unhappy about what was happening to them. She'd gone to see a therapist and had begun to learn that, despite her anger and resentment at being taken for granted—first by her parents, then by Richard and Leonard—she was still worthy of being loved.

Misty and Leonard had stayed together for a year and a half, and Misty had to admit that she preferred a man like Leonard to one like Richard. But since neither man was a prize, she decided that men weren't for her. In her opinion, love didn't liberate; it enslaved. Frequently she pondered the thought that her parents' love for her had begun to fade when she'd become a teenager and demanded control of her own destiny.

Sometimes she could still hear her father shouting, "Slut! That's what you are—a slut! It's after midnight, young lady."

"Hey, lady, what's the matter? You sick or somethin'? This is your address."

Misty clapped her hand over her mouth to stifle a groan. "Ah, it's nothing," she told the cab driver. "Just thinking. Here you are." She handed over some money. "Keep the change."

Misty climbed out of the cab and trudged up the stoop

to the front door of the brownstone she owned with four other people. She'd been delighted when, after leaving Leonard, she'd learned that the small stock investment her uncle had made for her had grown into enough money to buy a good-sized co-op apartment. At a time in her life when her problems had loomed large, owning her own home had given her a sense of security. But tonight she was too weary to appreciate the joys of ownership.

As she often did, Misty climbed the four flights of stairs instead of using the tiny elevator, which made her feel claustrophobic. The exercise was good for her heart, she told herself. Besides, it made her tired, let her sleep.

Her apartment was on the top floor, a sunny studio with a wall of windows at the back. Best of all, a previous occupant had soundproofed the walls and floor so that she could practice her piano at any hour of the day or night without disturbing the other tenants. She'd bought the piano at a household auction in Connecticut and paid a king's ransom to have it hoisted up the rear of the building and through a window. She'd been broke for months afterward.

That night, instead of going straight to bed, she decided to play the piano before trying to sleep. After locking the door and slipping off her shoes, she crossed her frugally furnished apartment, sighing with pleasure as her feet sank into the soft Oriental rug covering the hardwood floor. Except for the rug and piano, the only other piece of furniture was the king-sized water bed she had purchased from the previous apartment owners. It had taken her weeks to adjust to the bed, but now she enjoyed it.

At the floor-to-ceiling windows Misty had hung a green curtain of plants. Across the floor she'd scattered colorful throw cushions. She could lower the rope blinds over the windows when she wanted privacy, but more often she pulled them up to let in as much of the scarce Manhattan sunlight as possible.

It was still dark, however, as Misty sat down at the piano and played every piece of classical music she knew from memory. She played to exorcise both Richard's and Leonard's ghosts from her life. In the last few months she had come to realize that in many ways both men were like her father. They had seen her not as she was or could be, but as a reflection of their own desires.

Misty's hands came down on a discordant arpeggio. She wanted no more men in her life! Lucas Stuyvesant Harrison was just like all the others, and she wanted no part of him.

Her fingers were once more poised over the keys when an image of the man rose before her. His brown eyes glittered with the hardness of granite. His ash blond hair flashed silver under the artificial light. His impeccably tailored tuxedo conformed to every muscle in his tall, lean form.

"Stop it. Stop it, Misty," she admonished herself. "Wipe him out of your mind. He's trouble. Your life is just beginning to be your own. You have a good job. You can pay your bills. You're playing the piano every day, and you get occasional orchestral jobs." Reciting the familiar litany of blessings in her life helped her to feel less anxious, less alone.

When the orange light of dawn filtered through the windows, Misty went to bed, falling instantly into a deep and dreamless sleep.

She awoke thinking the building was coming down around her. A terrible noise filled her ears. As her eyes popped open, it took her a moment to realize that someone was banging on her door.

"Misty! Misty, did you forget the twins' lesson today?" Aileen Collins called out. Aileen and her husband David lived on the parlor floor with their ten-year-old twins, Mark and Mary.

"Huh?" Misty sat up in bed, blinking and running a hand absently through her tangled hair. "Oh, wait, Aileen. I'm coming." She jumped out of bed, her flannel nightgown falling to her ankles as she staggered over to the door and unlocked it. "Sorry. I overslept."

She smiled groggily at her friend and the exuberant twins, who called out "Hi, Misty!" and bounded past her into the room. Heading straight for the water bed, they tumbled into the center amid squeals of laughter.

"Stop that, now!" Aileen called, rolling her eyes in exasperation. "I should have kept them downstairs. I'll bet you haven't even been to bed yet."

"Yes, I slept for several hours. Why don't you make me

some coffee, and I'll start Mary on her scales?"

"Done." Aileen grinned, but she couldn't quite mask her concern for her friend.

"Now, don't start mothering me again," Misty protested. "I'm fine. I don't need much sleep. I told you that." She laughed, moving toward the piano bench.

"But there's a great deal you've never told me about yourself, Misty," Aileen said softly. When her friend didn't answer, she shrugged and went into the small kitchen to fill the electric drip pot with coffee.

Misty showed Mary where to start in the *Dozen a Day* book of finger exercises for beginners and listened attentively as her pupil began to play. Misty was grateful for the income from these weekly lessons, which helped pay her bills each month. She also knew Aileen was delighted that her children didn't have to travel for the lessons she and David wanted them to have.

The hour passed quickly. Afterward, Misty and Aileen chatted over another cup of coffee while the children drank milk and munched cookies that Misty stocked especially for them.

"So, how was it last night?" Aileen asked, keeping a close eye on the twins, who were wrangling over a game on the oval carpet.

Misty shrugged. "The usual Christmas party scene. People getting drunk, laughing too loudly." She paused. "But at least they were all chauffeured home after this gathering. The boss arranged it."

"Oh? Who's the boss?"

"Lucas Stuyvesant Harrison. Isn't that some name?"

Aileen whistled. "I've seen his picture in the paper lots of times. That man has a veritable stable of women. I read in a gossip column that he has no intention of marrying anyone from outside his social circle. Keeping up the family name, don't you know?" Aileen curled her pinky finger and raised her cup in an exaggerated imitation of a pretentious person.

"Ah, yes, noblesse oblige." Misty grinned, but she could feel her stomach contract. Undoubtedly Luc Harrison had thought she would be eager to join his stable of women. She should be pleased to think he might want to set her up in an apartment, give her clothes, deign to see her on Wednesdays, perhaps even on Thursdays—but never on weekends. He must save those for the family, the little woman.

"Hey, what are you thinking, Misty? I can almost hear your red hair crackling with anger. Your eyes are sparkling like emeralds. What's going through your mind?" Aileen leaned eagerly forward, her chin in her hand.

"Nothing. That type of man irritates me, that's all."

Aileen shrugged. "He's got everything—money, women, a great position with the bank. He's sailed in the America's Cup race. He's a scratch golfer. He's even competed in the triathlon in Hawaii, and you have to be in superb shape to do that. You have to swim, run, and ride a bike twelve miles without stopping in between." Aileen refilled her coffee cup and added cream. "I suppose a man with that kind of record comes to expect good things to tumble into his lap." She smiled at Misty. "I know you've sworn off men for some reason." When Misty began to protest, Aileen held up her hand, palm outward. "And, no, I'm not prying again. I admit I'd like to know, but I'll wait until you're ready to tell me."

I'll never be ready, Misty thought. *Even though you are the best friend I've ever had, I can't tell you.*

"But it wouldn't hurt to flirt a little with a man like Luc Harrison," Aileen added.

"I doubt I'll see him again," Misty said. "He came with his staff for the party. He won't be back. Men like him go to private clubs."

Aileen shook her head. "Don't sell the Terrace Hotel short. Some of the most influential people in the world stay there. David says you can walk into the Elm Bar any night and see celebrities. From what you've said, quite a few frequent the Edwardian Room as well."

"Quite a few," Misty conceded.

She and Aileen talked of other things. Then Aileen rounded up the twins and said good-bye. Misty was tired by the time they left, but instead of going back to bed, she straightened the apartment, showered, and shampooed her hair. She was due for a fitting at Morey Weinstein's design studio downtown that afternoon, so she wouldn't have time for a nap. If Morey didn't have any clothes ready for her to try on, she'd shop for shoes and accessories instead. Morey designed most of the clothes she wore while performing. Although he wasn't a commercial success yet, Misty had no doubt he would be someday.

Misty left her apartment at three o'clock that afternoon, knowing she wouldn't be back until three the next morning. She shook her head, trying not to think of the fatigue that would soon weigh on her like an iron blanket. Luckily she had tomorrow night off.

It took Misty half an hour to get to Morey's garretlike studio on the top floor of a run-down building encrusted with grime. Morey had every intention of moving uptown one day, and Misty was sure that, considering his talent, he would eventually make it.

She rang the bell adjacent to a locked oak door and submitted to being scrutinized by an eye at the peephole. The eye disappeared, and the door was swung open by a whipcord-thin man of medium height who radiated energy and enthusiasm.

"Mystique! I've been thinking about you for two days. If you hadn't come this afternoon I was going to call you. I found some fabulous silk." Morey shoved his black-rimmed glasses up his nose with an index finger and grinned, his pale blue eyes sparkling with excitement.

"Silk, Morey? I can't afford silk. For that matter, neither can you." Misty laughed as her irrepressible friend tugged her across his littered workroom to the cutting board under the skylight.

"True," he conceded. "But this was water-damaged, so Fetler let me have it for almost nothing." He grinned and waved his hand when she frowned. "Now, don't worry. Fetler didn't bother to unravel the bolts. I did. The damage doesn't go through all the way. This is great stuff—the finest silk from Japan. Look at the colors—blue, green, burgundy, orange, cerise, lemon." He let out an ecstatic sigh as Misty bent over the material.

"It *is* beautiful," she agreed, "but I can't afford to pay you what it's worth."

"Listen, Misty, don't worry. The clients you've sent to me have a lot of friends. My business is really picking up.

I've hired two women to sew, and"—he paused, clasping his hands together—"there's a good chance I might get into that building I was telling you about, the one uptown. I could live in the apartment off the main room."

"Oh, Morey, that's great!" Misty gave her friend an enthusiastic hug.

"Now, don't get too excited. I haven't talked with the bank yet, and Manhattan Stuyvesant is tough on this sort of thing, especially since my only collateral is my talent."

"But that's very big collateral," Misty assured him.

Morey's expression became momentarily woebegone. "I hope the bank thinks so." Then he brightened. "Come on, get undressed. I want to see this stuff on you."

When Misty arrived at the Terrace Hotel for work that evening she was already bone tired. Morey had pinned, pulled, and draped material on her until she couldn't stand another moment. But by the middle of next week their efforts would pay off when she became the proud owner of two lovely silk gowns. The cost wouldn't even put too much of a hole in her savings. She shouldn't let Morey sell the dresses to her too cheaply, she thought as she took a black satin gown and matching pumps from her carrier. But she also realized she would never be able to afford them if he didn't give her a good deal. He was such a good friend.

That evening she played for a smaller Christmas party than the night before. "Thank God, this is the last of them," Willis commented wearily during her break.

"Amen to that. Only three days to Christmas, and I haven't put up my tree or finished my shopping."

Willis laughed and shook his head. "My wife takes care of that."

"Lucky you."

Misty left the hotel at two-thirty the next morning. Her head was throbbing painfully because she'd skipped dinner. Fatigue clung to her like wet cement, making every movement an ordeal.

At home, she barely took time to hang up her clothes and put away her dress carrier before she tumbled into bed and down, down into the well of sleep.

Hours later, the insistent peal of the telephone jarred her

awake. She blinked at the clock on her bedside table and was stunned to see that it was four in the afternoon. Her day off was almost gone. At least she had the evening to herself. "'Lo?" she said groggily.

"Misty, it's Morey. The bank turned me down!" Her friend's anguish came through to her with painful clarity.

"Oh, no! They couldn't have. How could they be so stupid?" Misty sat up in bed and pushed back her thick hair. "Did they give you a reason?"

"It seems I need more collateral than my talent." Morey tried to laugh, but Misty heard the heartache in his voice.

"Listen, Morey, don't give up yet. I'll put up my apartment as collateral. It's the least I can do after all your kindness to me. Let me help you out. Please."

"Misty, I can't. Your apartment is all you have."

"Please let me. I'll become your silent partner. Weinstein Couturiers must survive. Please. I want to do it."

"Misty . . ." Morey's voice cracked. "Except for Zena, you're the best friend I've ever had." As soon as his business was well established, Morey planned to marry Zena, who worked as an assistant wardrobe mistress in a downtown theater.

"It's too late to go to the bank today," Misty went on, "but we'll be there waiting when the doors open tomorrow."

When they walked into the awesome foyer of the Manhattan Stuyvesant Bank early the next morning, Misty stared admiringly at the three-story vaulted ceiling decorated with mosaic tiles in intricate patterns. Offices on the second and third floors opened onto a horseshoe-shaped balcony that afforded a clear view of activity on the main floor, with its long row of tellers' windows and intimate groupings of officers' desks and chairs. The open space and hum of subdued voices created a hushed, formal atmosphere.

"The silence is intimidating," Misty whispered with an uneasy smile.

"If you think you're intimidated now, wait until you meet Mr. Watson." Morey ushered her over to a chair. "We have to wait our turn," he explained.

Twenty minutes ticked by. Misty began to fidget. She kept getting the feeling that someone was watching her. But when she glanced around the bank and up to the second- and third-story balconies, she saw no one looking her way.

Finally, after they'd waited for thirty-five minutes, Mr. Watson ushered them to his desk on which a discreet sign said: Loan Information. They all sat down. "Now then, Mr. Weinstein," Mr. Watson began, "you said you wanted to see me again. I must tell you, however, that I don't think we can change our minds on this—" The phone rang, interrupting him. "Excuse me." Morey and Misty exchanged glances as Mr. Watson picked up the receiver. "Ah, good morning, sir." Mr. Watson sat straighter in his chair. "Yes, yes. A loan. Ah, no collateral." Mr. Watson shot a quick glance at Morey.

"But he has collateral—my apartment," Misty exclaimed, jumping out of her chair and leaning across Mr. Watson's desk.

Mr. Watson appeared to be taken aback by her forwardness. He quickly covered the mouthpiece of the phone and directed a quelling look at Misty, then spoke quickly. "Ah . . . I'm sorry, sir. No, there's no need for you— You want me to what? You're coming down here?" Mr. Watson finished weakly and stared at the receiver with a baffled expression. "He hung up," he muttered.

"Who?" Misty asked, still standing.

"Huh? Ah . . . never mind. What were you saying about your apartment? There could be extenuating circumstances." Mr. Watson took the papers Misty handed him and began perusing them, but his thoughts were obviously elsewhere. Several times he looked anxiously up toward the second-floor balcony. Then abruptly he jumped to his feet, his gaze going past Misty and a disconsolate Morey to a distinguished-looking man in a three-piece suit. "Mr. Damon, sir. Did Mr.—"

"Never mind, John, I'll take care of this," the man said. "Perhaps you could attend to the next person. Why don't you use another desk?"

"Of course." Mr. Watson sprung away from his chair and hurried toward an elderly couple sitting nervously some distance away in the cavernous lobby.

"Hello, I'm Lester Damon," the man greeted them. He shook Misty's hand, then Morey's. "Sit down, please, Miss

Carver. I'll just take a look at Mr. Weinstein's papers."
Silence fell as Lester Damon perused the sheets in front of
him. At length he paused and looked up. "Miss Carver, do
you plan to put up your apartment as collateral, so that you
will, in effect, become partners with Mr. Weinstein?" he
asked.

"Yes." Misty met Lester Damon's direct gaze without
flinching, but she had a terrible feeling that he was going
to turn them down. Why hadn't he let Mr. Watson consider
their loan application? Why was he stringing them along?
Her temper was beginning to rise.

But to her surprise, Lester Damon said, "Fine. Everything seems to be in order." He pushed the papers toward
Morey. "You have your loan, Mr. Weinstein."

"I do?" "He does?" Morey and Misty croaked in unison.

"It's all set," Mr. Damon assured them, shaking their
flaccid hands. "If you have any problems, Mr. Weinstein,
please call me. Don't bother going through Mr. Watson.
But I don't think you'll run into any difficulties. Pick up
your check from Miss Edwards at the cashier's desk. Good
day." Mr. Damon smiled at each of them, then strode swiftly
away.

Morey fell back into his chair. "I think I'm hyperven-
tilating," he wheezed, loosening his tie with trembling fingers.

"I'm having a little trouble myself," Misty whispered
back. "Come on," she said, urging her friend to his feet.
"Let's get out of here. Don't forget that stamped paper.
Let's pick up the check; then we'll call Zena and celebrate."

"Lord, Misty. Maybe Zena and I can get married this
year after all," Morey said in trembling tones as they approached a smiling woman behind a desk.

Minutes later, they left the bank arm in arm. Misty had
the feeling that at any moment Mr. Damon would come
rushing after them and declare that it was all a mistake.
"Hurry, Morey." She urged him along the street to the bus
stop, not pausing to take a breath until they were on the bus
and several blocks from the Manhattan Stuyvesant Bank.
They called Zena from Morey's apartment and agreed to
meet her for lunch at a nearby deli.

Morey insisted on buying the lox and cream cheese. Zena

sniffled all through the meal.

"Zena, honey, stop crying," Morey pleaded. "There's a policeman over there who keeps staring at me."

"I will, I will," she promised tearfully, kissing his cheek and turning grateful eyes to Misty. "You're the best friend we ever had, Misty. Thank you."

"Thank *you*. Not many people will have the privilege of saying 'I knew Morey and Zena Weinstein before they were famous.' But *I* will." She grinned happily at her two friends.

After lunch, Misty shopped for Christmas presents. She was delighted when she found a scarf for Aileen, a word game for Mark, and a stuffed animal for Mary. For Morey and Zena she bought a starter set of china in a pattern they had admired. She sent a poinsettia to her aunt and uncle at their new home in Florida. Since her mother and father had returned every gift she'd sent them, she planned to mail them a check. For her sister Celia she bought a chess set; for Marcy she bought tapes of the latest rock music; for Betsy, the youngest, she'd already bought a hand-crocheted vest at a church bazaar. Though she always tried to choose gifts her sisters would enjoy, she never really knew if they liked them. Her mother's terse thank-you note never provided details. Misty had buried her hurt so long ago that she rarely dwelt on it now. On her way home, she selected a small Douglas fir tree from a corner vendor.

Back at her apartment she just had time to set the tree in a container filled with water before she had to get ready for work.

The Edwardian Room was crowded that night, only two days before Christmas. A sense of anticipation filled the air, and Misty willingly immersed herself in her music. Then, abruptly, unaccountably, she stiffened and raised her eyes.

Lucas Harrison was sitting at a table directly in her line of vision. His eyes met hers for a brief, intense moment before she looked hastily away. From then on, whenever she looked up, she found his gaze riveted on her.

During her break she gestured to Willis with a shake of her head. "Isn't it a comedown for the director of the Manhattan Stuyvesant Bank to be here?" she asked.

Willis gave her a knowing look. "He's been here three

times since the Christmas party. Last night, when he heard you were off, he left right away. Usually he asks for a table in the back where you can't see him."

Misty was stunned. "He's been here every evening since the party?" she repeated incredulously.

"Yes. For at least an hour each night." Willis moved away to greet a couple who had been hovering at the entrance to the Edwardian Room.

Misty continued to play, but her head was filled with the fact that Luc Harrison had come to watch her play the piano several times.

During her break she strolled to the powder room, then to her usual place at the Elm Bar. She had just sat down when she felt the press of silken material against her bare back.

"Let me buy you a drink, Mystique."

She didn't bother to turn around. "All right. I'd like mineral water with lime, please."

Luc Harrison gave the bartender her order and his own for an Old Bushmills on the rocks. Once the drinks were in front of them he said casually, "You play very well."

"Thank you." Misty took a gulp of the cool drink and coughed when it went down the wrong way.

"Are you going to face me at all?" the voice asked, "or are we going to converse by looking at our images in the mirror?"

Misty's eyes flew to the reflection over the bar and caught the saturnine look on his face. "It's not necessarily a bad way to converse," she said.

"No, but I prefer the more personal way—face to face." He moved between her stool and the waitresses' pickup station. They were so close that their legs bumped. She only had to lift her eyes a few inches to meet his gaze.

Misty took a deep breath as his eyes scanned hers. A tingling sensation ran through her body. "I . . . I was in your bank today, the main one downtown. It's beautiful."

"Yes. It's an architectural marvel—or so the brochures describe it to sightseers."

"My friend procured a loan to move his business to a better location," Misty explained, glad to have found a safe topic of conversation.

"Is he your lover or just a platonic friend?" Luc queried smoothly.

The question surprised her. "What difference does that make?"

"None." The terse answer seemed to linger between them. The silence grew heavy.

"At first your bank turned down my friend's loan application," Misty said, feeling increasingly uncomfortable. She cleared her throat nervously.

"I know. I saw you at the bank today."

She stared at him, stunned. He was looking straight ahead into the mirror. "I had a feeling someone was watching me," she blurted out.

"I had come out of Lester Damon's office on the third floor and was waiting for the elevator when I happened to look down and see you."

"So, you sent Mr. Damon down to—"

"I called Watson from my office. Then I told Les to go down and handle it. John Watson is an honest man, but he would have required too many explanations, and he probably wouldn't have issued you the check."

"But I had collateral."

"Do you really think that one-fourth of a brownstone is equal in value to the third floor of the Beadle Building?"

She lifted her chin. "My apartment is worth a great deal more now than it was when I bought it. The neighborhood is good and—"

"And the entire building isn't worth a quarter of the Beadle property." Luc took a swallow of his Irish whisky and ran a finger slowly up her bare arm.

She stiffened at his touch. "I have to get back. My break is over," she managed to say. Her body felt both hot and cold. She felt both threatened and titillated. She had to escape!

Luc took hold of her upper arm and scrutinized her through narrowed eyes, a hard smile lifting his lips. "Yes, to your unspoken question, Mystique. I do want something from you in return for granting you that loan."

Cold dread pierced through to her very core. She raised stricken eyes to his, then fled as if all the demons of hell were at her heels.

CHAPTER TWO

WHEN MISTY WOKE up the next morning, Christmas Eve, the first thing that entered her mind was Luc's statement from the previous evening: *"I do want something from you..."*

Somehow she had managed to return to the Edwardian Room and continue to play the piano, but she had felt like a whirling dervish. Her thoughts had flown in all directions, and she hadn't been able to concentrate. At some point she had become aware that Luc Harrison was no longer at his table. She hadn't felt relieved or glad, just numb.

Now, the next morning, she wished for the hundredth time that she didn't have to work on Christmas Eve and Christmas night. At the time her schedule had been drawn up, she hadn't cared that she would be working those two nights. But now she was sorely tempted to quit her job and hide from Luc Harrison.

Stop it, Misty Carver, she told herself silently. Chances were Luc Harrison wouldn't show up either night. He had a huge family, and he would spend the holidays with them.

Feeling somewhat mollified, she cleaned her apartment

and began to prepare the buffet supper she would serve that evening for Dave and Aileen, Mark and Mary, Morey and Zena. Tomorrow she would join Dave and Aileen for dinner in their apartment.

Several times during the day the twins came charging up the stairs to look at the gifts under Misty's tree, their faces alight with excitement. "I like it when Morey and Zena come," Mark informed her, "'cause we go to their place for Hanniker, and we get gifts both times."

"Chanukah," Misty corrected absently as she arranged gumdrops into an edible wreath for the center of the table. She would put a fat bayberry candle in the middle. "You're lucky children to be able to join in both the Jewish and the Christian holidays. You can learn a lot from both traditions."

"Yes," Mary said solemnly. "You get the best foods on the holidays."

"Yes, dear," Misty agreed. "Mark, don't you dare shake one more package."

"Awww, Misty . . ."

"On your way now the two of you. Take your baths and get dressed. You'll be going to church with your parents after we have our supper."

"Why aren't you going to services with us, Misty?" Mary asked, tearing her gaze from the gumdrop wreath. "Are you Jewish like Zena and Morey?"

"No, she's working." Mark tapped his sister on the arm. "Race you downstairs."

"Nooo," Mary said with a moan as her brother raced out the door. She turned to Misty with a smile. "I always say no, but he never listens. Now I'll walk down real slow, and he'll think he's won the race." Mary's curls bobbed as she walked primly out of the room.

"How did you get to be so wise, Mary?" Misty asked softly. She was glad the twins had been around to distract her all day. They had kept her from thinking about Luc Harrison. She refused to consider what he might want from her. She was pretty sure she knew . . . and she was damn sure he wasn't going to get it.

Promptly at five, Misty's guests arrived. After coaxing and cajoling the twins into eating dinner *before* opening their presents, they all filled their plates with hot antipasto; cold prawns in hot sauce; and then pasta shells stuffed with ricotta, parsley, and sausage.

"I'd love to have some of these make-ahead recipes, Misty," Zena said, closing her eyes in delight as she tasted a stuffed shell.

"All my recipes are for dishes you can make ahead," Misty said, laughing. "That's the only kind I have time to prepare."

They all ate their fill, then settled down on cushions around the tree and opened their gifts over coffee, a fruit board, and Christmas cookies. Misty had such a good time that, long after her guests had departed, she felt as if she were floating on happiness. She hummed Christmas carols as she got ready for work and ran lightly downstairs and outside to hail a cab. Christmas Eve had been wonderful. She refused to allow the fact that she hadn't heard from either of her parents to dull her delight.

At the hotel, Misty passed out the gifts she had bought for her friends on the staff. She laughed when Willis put on his Australian wool sweater vest right over his shirt. "You can't wear your tuxedo jacket over a sweater," she protested, laughing.

"It's Christmas Eve. Of course I can," he insisted. "Thank you for the sweater, Misty. I love blue."

"And thank you for the lace hankies, Willis. Tell your wife they're just perfect to carry with the gowns I wear. My hands get damp when I play, but I'll look very ladylike using these hankies to discreetly wipe my palms."

That night Misty played some of her usual songs, but she concentrated on playing Christmas carols. She didn't think of Luc Harrison until she caught sight of his tuxedo-clad form entering the Edwardian Room. Her fingers faltered momentarily, and she hit a B-flat instead of an A-natural, but other than that she made no sign that she had noticed him.

During her break, she went directly to the powder room and stayed there until it was time to return to the piano.

As she sat down again to play, she saw a hand place a glass on the frame of the piano, where the mahogany surface was protected by a metal tray.

"Thank you, Willis," she said without looking up. "I was thirsty."

"I thought you might be," came Luc Harrison's velvet voice. Her eyes shot up to his granite-hard eyes.

"Merry Christmas," she managed to say through stiff lips. She watched dumbfounded as he placed a small package wrapped in silver paper on the piano, then turned and strode from the room before she could speak again.

Misty looked at the gift as though she expected it to explode at any moment.

"What's this? A gift from a fan?" Willis hefted the small package in his palm.

"You could say that." Misty smiled weakly and bent over the keyboard.

As usual, she was exhausted when she returned to her apartment very early Christmas morning. Yet, despite her fatigue, she was too keyed up and apprehensive to sleep. She felt as though she were carrying a time bomb in her purse instead of a very small package.

She stripped off her clothes, brushed down the green velvet dress she had worn that evening, and hung it in the bathroom where it would steam the next time she showered. She had learned to take good care of her clothing; she couldn't easily afford to replace it.

After putting away her clothes and shoes, she donned a flannel nightgown and crawled into the middle of the water bed, where she sat cross-legged and stared at her purse. Swallowing twice, she unzipped the bag and reached for the gift inside, holding it in her palm for a moment before inserting a fingernail carefully under the wrapping. That was another of her economies; she saved paper and bows.

After folding the paper along its crease lines, she rolled up the ribbon and stared at the box. The name Van Cleef & Arpels was printed across the top.

No doubt he had a charge account there, she thought. Calls up and orders a gross of aquamarines and sends them to his friends. Millimeter by millimeter she lifted the hinged cover. Her eyes grew wide. "Good God!" she exclaimed softly, blinking at the sight of emerald earrings arranged on apricot velvet. How dare he give her something so expensive? Did he think she was too stupid to know he was coming on to her with jewelry? She scooted back on the bed, putting as much distance as possible between herself and the exquisite jewels.

It took several minutes to get up the courage to lean forward and pull the box toward her. With great care she rewrapped the package and dropped it back into her purse.

Anger made her writhe and turn on her bed until dawn. Finally she fell into a fitful sleep. Her last thought was that no man was ever going to take charge of her life again.

Christmas Day brought laughter, good food, and several more small gifts for the twins, despite their parents' mild protests. As Misty played Christmas songs on the Collinses' spinet, they all sang, ate, and laughed.

Afterward, Aileen handed her a glass of eggnog. "I could swear I heard your phone ringing. You know how the sound sometimes vibrates in the old dumbwaiter. Even though we can't hear anything else, I sometimes hear the phone. Do you suppose you should go up and answer it?"

Misty hesitated. No, it wouldn't be her parents. They never called her. She would call them before she went to work that evening. "No, I won't bother," she said. "It's probably a wrong number."

She returned to her apartment in the early evening. Morey and Zena would be staying awhile longer with David and Aileen, and the twins were already in bed sound asleep.

That night the Edwardian Room was full to capacity with complete families as well as couples. Misty saw a few single people dining alone, and she tried to play just for them. She could empathize with their loneliness.

All evening she kept a sharp eye out for a tall masculine form. Even during her break she searched the corners of the room that she couldn't see while playing. She was determined to return Lucas Harrison's gift.

"Looking for someone, Mystique?" Willis asked with a smile.

"Just checking the numbers," she said, hedging.

Luc Harrison never came. Once again, Misty went home with the expensive emeralds in her purse.

She carried them twice more to the Terrace Hotel. Then, on the third day, she wrapped the package in brown paper, put it in a sturdy mailing envelope addressed to the Manhattan Stuyvesant Bank's main office, and carried it to the post office. Just before mailing it she wrote *Personal* on the front.

Since she had to work on New Year's Eve, she had wrangled special holiday reservations for Morey and Zena, Aileen and David. Neither of the couples planned to take advantage of the overnight accommodations or the breakfast, which had cut down on the cost for Misty. It delighted her to be able to do something extra for her friends, who had done so much for her, and she refused to take any money from David or Morey when they tried to press it on her.

How could they know what a relief it would be to have them with her on what was for her the worst night of the year? Misty mused when she arrived that evening for work. New Year's Eve was a night for couples. She was single. It hurt, but she was determined not to show it.

As she changed in her small dressing room, a niggling thought chased through her mind. Had Luc Harrison received the emeralds in the mail? She had insured them, but she was certain they were worth more than the maximum insurance the post office had allowed her. She felt as though she were waiting for the other shoe to drop. She didn't know what was worse—not seeing him and not knowing if he had received the jewels, or seeing him and knowing. She shook her head to clear it of such thoughts and studied her reflection in the narrow mirror on the back of the door. Morey was right. Her new silk dress was perfect.

The emerald green fabric was draped around her like a sari, delineating her lissome form in glittering silkiness as the faint gold thread caught the light. Her curly red hair was pulled to one side with an ivory comb, the tousled locks catching gold fire in the light. The four-inch heels of her pale green peau de soie pumps made her a svelte five feet eight inches tall.

As she studied herself, she felt an unusual surge of confidence, but immediately chided herself. She'd felt like that before and fallen flat on her face. She'd better be careful.

As she left the dressing room, she heard sounds of revelry coming from the Elm Bar. The rooms were already filling up for the partygoers' biggest night of the year.

Misty was stopped several times on her short walk to the Edwardian Room by men who had already had several drinks. Two men even tried to kiss her, but she easily eluded them, smiling good-naturedly.

"Happy New Year, Mystique," Willis greeted her. "We're almost filled already." It was only a few minutes before nine.

"Happy New Year, Willis." Misty smiled back at him and walked over to the piano. Before sitting down she scanned the room. She caught sight of Morey and Zena waving. David and Aileen hadn't arrived yet. No doubt they'd had to wait for the sitter. Then her casual gaze fell on a crowded table almost directly in front of her. Luc Harrison sat there facing her. He lifted his glass in a silent salute, and Misty shivered at the hard look in his eyes.

Immediately she began to play, hoping to lose herself in the music. Luc Harrison couldn't possibly harm her here at the Terrace Hotel. She was safe for now.

The room seemed to be seething with loud, laughing people. More than one man came up to the piano and asked her to play a special song. She always complied.

One minute time seemed to be crawling by; the next, she realized an hour had passed since she'd last checked her watch.

At eleven-thirty Misty took a break, knowing she would have to play "Auld Lang Syne" at midnight.

She left the piano and made her way past the tables to where her four friends were sitting. Passing Luc Harrison's table, she thought she heard a low comment aimed in her direction: "God, she's lovely. Why not come over here, pretty redhead?"

She wasn't sure, but she thought she heard Luc mutter a sharp reply.

"Hi," Aileen said, beaming. "This is too beautiful for words, Misty. And guess what? Our baby-sitter is going to spend the night so we can stay as late as we want. Isn't that great?"

"Wonderful," Misty agreed, squeezing into a chair and accepting the drink that one of the waiters brought to the table.

"You look gorgeous in that dress, Misty," Zena said with a sigh.

"And I'll have you know that several women have approached me tonight and asked where I buy my clothes. I told them, of course." The others laughed with her.

Morey poured her champagne, but she shook her head. "I really shouldn't. I'll get a headache, and I'm on until five in the morning." She held up her own glass. "Tomato juice. This will give me the energy I need. Say, why don't the four of you come up to the piano at midnight? Then I won't have to race down here to give you your New Year's kisses."

"Great!" David exclaimed.

Misty glanced at her watch. "Oops! Ten minutes. I have to go. In about five minutes, come on up." She rose and made her way back to the piano, staying well away from the table where Luc Harrison was sitting.

Minutes later, people began counting down the time.

From the corner of her eye Misty saw her friends rise from their table and move toward her. As she sent them a bright smile, she caught sight of Luc Harrison scrutinizing them for a fleeting moment before looking back at her. Then she was too busy to register anything but the guests counting down the seconds until midnight.

"Ten . . . nine . . . eight . . . seven," they shouted. "Five . . . four . . . three . . . two . . . one! Happy New Year!"

Misty laughed along with everyone else, nodding happily as her friends hugged her and her fingers moved over the keyboard. As soon as she finished playing "Auld Lang Syne," she jumped up and kissed Zena, Aileen, David, Morey . . .

"Happy New Year, darling." A masculine mouth covered hers as Luc spoke the words, his breath going into her mouth, his tongue touching her teeth, then her tongue.

Misty tried to suck in air, to release herself from his embrace, but all at once she felt herself free-falling through space, detached from her own body, wrapped in an aura of throbbing delight. She pressed closer to him and heard a groan come from deep inside her, then his answering growl of pleasure.

Misty fell back, ending the kiss, her eyes darting around her. Had anyone seen the soul-stirring kiss she and Luc

Harrison had just exchanged? People were laughing, hugging, joking. Her eyes shot back to him. His face darkened as he bent over her, his sensual mouth not an inch away, his brown eyes burning into her.

"I knew it would be like that, but it was even better than I imagined. You're wonderful." His hand brushed downward over her breast. "You shouldn't have sent your gift back. The earrings belong to you. They're so like your eyes," he whispered.

"No," Misty croaked out. "I don't want anything from you. Get away from my piano. I have to play."

She ran her hands up and down the keyboard and then broke into "Auld Lang Syne" once again.

Gradually people stopped talking and kissing, and faced the piano. Their party hats askew, they began to sing the words of the Robert Burns poem, the poignant lines touching Misty deeply.

She played the song at least four times, until everyone had had a chance to sing at the piano. Then the dancing began. As usual on special occasions, she had the support of two backup musicians, Roddy on drums and Lem on bass.

She was glad to be distracted by her music. She didn't look at Luc Harrison at all, though at intervals she looked up and smiled into the audience. When the set ended, she went straight to her friends' table, where she sat and talked with them.

At three-thirty in the morning her friends rose to leave. They came up to the piano to say good night.

"I won't bother to call you for breakfast . . . or brunch . . . or dinner," Aileen said, yawning and leaning on David. "But I have to tell you that this has been one memorable New Year's Eve. Thank you, Misty."

"Yes, thank you, Misty. And you look beautiful in my dress." Morey kissed her on the lips, as did David. Then the four of them were gone.

"Happy New Year," Misty whispered after them, more grateful than she could say for their presence there tonight.

She watched the crowd dwindle, though several groups remained until after four-thirty. She felt both relief and emptiness when she saw Luc Harrison's party depart. No doubt he and his date would stay in one of the best suites and have breakfast in bed, then a nice long sleep . . . in the same bed. She was glad she hadn't been able to figure which of the women at the Harrison table had been Luc's date.

At ten minutes to five on New Year's morning, the Edwardian Room was empty except for a few busboys and waiters. Misty said good night to her backup men and leaned against the piano for a moment, rubbing her throbbing temples. It had been a long night.

"Tired, darling?" Luc Harrison crooned, his hand slipping around her waist. "Come on. I have some food ready for you."

Misty blinked up at him. "I'm not hungry." She hadn't sampled food from the buffet because she played better on an empty stomach.

"You didn't eat anything tonight," he told her firmly, leading her from the room.

"I don't want to go anywhere. I'm exhausted."

"We'll eat right here," he reassured her.

"You're crazy. The dining rooms are closed for the night."

"We'll eat in my suite upstairs."

"I'm not joining your floozies!" Misty sputtered as he led her into an elevator. He inserted a key into a slot and pressed the top button on the panel. "You have the penthouse suite. That's disgusting." Misty lifted a hand to cover her yawn. "I'm not staying. I have to get some sleep." She struggled against him for a moment, then subsided. She just didn't have the strength to fight him. Exhaustion weakened her resolve to get to her dressing room, change, hail a cab, and go home.

"Fine. First you'll get a little nourishment," Luc said. "You can't live on tomato juice." He still had an arm around her when the elevator doors opened onto a small foyer.

Misty walked into the living room of the penthouse. She scanned the curving stairway that led to the second floor. She squinted at the table set for two in front of sliding glass doors that led onto a terrace. She noted the Christmas tree and sundry decorations outside. "Pretty . . . but I can't stay." She yawned again, feeling a bit weary.

Luc put her carrier down on a couch along with the fleece-lined velvet cape that Morey had designed for her. "This is quite nice," he said.

Misty glanced at him, trying to stifle another yawn. "My friend Morey designed it for me. He's fabulous." Fascinated, she watched Luc's eyes turn hard, and a muscle tightened in his jaw. "You change expressions like a chameleon," she said.

"Chameleons change color," he corrected tersely.

"Whatever." She shrugged and ambled over to the couch, where she sank down into the velvet depths, her eyes sliding shut.

"Is he the man you arranged the loan for? This Morey?" Luc demanded.

"Huh?" Misty's eyes blinked open. "Ah, yes. He's my special friend." She tried to focus her thoughts but couldn't. "I really have to go."

"I see . . ." Luc's voice sounded from far away. "Wake up. The food will be here in a moment."

Misty yawned widely and struggled to her feet as Luc took hold of her elbow. "Didn't you see Morey tonight?" She wet her dry lips with her tongue. "He and Zena and Aileen and David were there."

Luc guided her into a chair at the table and went to answer a knock on the door. A waiter entered the room, pushing a covered cart ahead of him. He laid out the dishes and was gone, like a wraith.

Misty looked fuzzily after him. "That was fast." She stared at the array of food, feeling all at once hungry. "I think I would like some of that soup." She watched Luc ladle some into a small bowl, her mouth watering. "Zena makes marvelous soup. She says the trick is to let the schmaltz rise to the top and skim it off." Misty sighed. "I'm sure she and Morey will be eating a great deal of soup until his business takes off. But at least they'll be able to get married now." She yawned again and rubbed her face. "Aren't you going to have some soup?" she asked as Luc continued to watch her, the silver ladle poised above the tureen.

"Ah, yes." He served himself, then cut each of them thick slices of warm bread. "So Morey is going to marry Zena?" he asked.

Misty nodded, spooning the hot chicken broth into her mouth, feeling warmth spread through her.

She ate four bowls of the broth, which surprised her. She'd never been especially fond of soup. But, barely able to keep her eyes open, she refused the casserole and the side dishes. "I really have to go," she mumbled, glancing around for her cape.

Luc stood up and helped her out of the chair. "Not yet. You're dead on your feet. Lie down for a bit. Then I'll take you home."

With an effort, she looked up at him. "I really shouldn't . . ." But her head flopped forward onto his chest.

"Just a short nap," he urged, reaching down to lift her into his arms. "You're such a tiny thing."

Misty felt the comforting motion of being jostled against his shoulder as he carried her into another room. Then, before she knew it, she was asleep.

When she woke, she ran her eyes around the gold and cream-colored room, then closed them again. She was still in a dream. Good. She was too tired to get up anyway. She snuggled back down under the covers, not questioning the great comfort of the bed, but wondering why her water bed wasn't undulating as it always did. She didn't even question the solid warmth at her back. After all, her water bed was heated. Grateful for the extra sleep, she burrowed deeper into the warmth, certain that she couldn't have heard someone groan.

Nevertheless, she opened her sleepy eyes and blinked once again at the cream and gold room. She lay perfectly still, trying to orient herself. "If I didn't know better, I would think I fell asleep in the Queen Victoria Dining Room," she muttered, the sheet up to her chin, her eyes registering each opulent article in the large bedroom. "I must be drunk."

"On tomato juice," a deep voice murmured in her ear.

She snapped her eyes shut in a futile effort to hide from the sudden horrible realization that she had gone to bed with Lucas Stuyvesant Harrison! Stunned, she kept her eyes tightly closed, wishing she could disappear. What a way to start the New Year! After all the promises she had made to herself about how she would live her life. This was awful! She'd had no intention of doing such a thing! Was she losing her mind?

She turned her head slowly and looked into glittering brown eyes so close to her own that she could see the tiny gold and green flecks in the irises.

"Happy New Year, darling." He leaned forward and kissed her, his mouth a gentle caress, his tongue a hot, questing spear that set fire to her bloodstream. His arm slid over her bare middle and pulled her to him. "I wanted you to wake up, love. I've been waiting."

"You mean we haven't . . . ah, made love—euphemistically speaking, that is?"

His eyes narrowed on her, the sparkle in them turning to a hard glitter. "No, we haven't made love—euphemistically speaking."

Misty let out her breath in a long sigh and rolled away from Luc's loose hold, out of bed, and to her feet, snatching up a blanket to cover herself. She fumbled awkwardly, and the blanket slipped, revealing a generous amount of skin.

She stood rigidly straight, almost naked, facing him, her chin up and her hands clenching and unclenching on the blanket. Her face flushed and her skin burned under Luc's hot gaze as his eyes traveled over her. She took deep breaths, trying to steady herself as he lay on his side watching her, the sheet barely covering his lower body. She couldn't seem to force her voice from her throat.

"Do I take it you're telling me no, my darling, even though we've spent the night in each other's arms?"

"That's right—and I'm not your darling." Misty forced the hoarse words from her throat, shivering not so much from cold as from nervous tension.

Luc saw her shudder and reached behind him for his robe. He tossed it to her. "Put it on, Mystique. It will keep you warmer than the blanket."

She slid her arms into the voluminous sleeves, which hung past her hands. Only when the belt was tied did she drop the blanket. "My clothes," she said, keeping her eyes on him as he pointed behind her. Without turning, she stepped backward.

His expression darkened. "From your cautious behavior

I gather you expect me to jump out of bed and rape you. For some reason you don't trust me, Mystique."

"And all men like you," she snapped, shooting a quick glance at her silk dress lying on a chair. "Where's my carrier?"

"Downstairs in the living room. Shall I get it?"

"No!" With effort she controlled her anger. She didn't want to see him out of bed, naked and...beautiful. She closed her mind to the thought.

"Dammit, stop that," he railed. "I said I wasn't going to rape you, and I'm not. I don't know what the hell kind of men you've been dealing with, but I'm not what you think." His anger raised goose bumps on her skin, and she backed away. "Dammit, stop it, I said. You think I was wrong to climb into bed with you. Well, I don't, and I sure as hell don't feel guilty because I'm attracted to you. I haven't done anything to hurt you."

She didn't stay to hear more. In a flash she raced out of the room and down the stairs to the living room, grabbed up her carrier, and looked around wildly for a place to change.

"Try the bathroom over there." Her eyes shot upward. Luc was standing on the balcony overlooking the living room, a cheroot in his hand, a lighter held to the cigar. He was naked.

"Thank you," Misty mumbled, sliding her eyes quickly away from his form. God, he was beautiful...

She got dressed in the bathroom, his brown eyes and ash blond hair filling her thoughts. No way! she told herself. No way would she get caught in that trap again.

After dressing hurriedly and combing her hair, she emerged from the bathroom.

Luc stood in the middle of the living room, dressed in brown cord jeans with a champagne silk shirt and brown vest. "I'll take you home," he said.

"No need," she retorted, clutching her carrier to her.

"I said I'll take you home, and I will."

"I'd rather go home alone. I'll call a cab."

He ran a hand angrily through his tousled hair. "Dammit, Mystique, what the hell is the matter with you? I'm sorry if I offended you. I thought I made it clear that I had no intention of hurting you. But I also have no intention of hiding my attraction."

"That's why you sent the earrings. Since I sent them back, you should have gotten the message."

A smile fluttered across his mouth. "Yes, you did send them back, damn you." He took several restless steps and turned to face her. "What does it take to convince you that I want a relationship with you?"

In her anger, the words popped out before she considered them. "Two things: a certificate from the Board of Health saying that you're free of disease, and a proposal of marriage."

For once she had caught Luc Harrison by surprise.

CHAPTER THREE

ALL THE WAY home in the cab and for the rest of the morning Misty couldn't get out of her mind the expressions that had crossed Luc Harrison's face when she'd answered his question. Shock and incredulity had been followed rapidly by contempt, anger, and finally icy disdain.

"I'm afraid marriage isn't what I had in mind," he'd told her coldly. Then he'd helped her with her cape, called down to the doorman to hold a taxi, and watched her walk into the elevator. Neither of them had said good-bye.

In the shower, as she shampooed her hair, she wondered if Luc Harrison really thought she expected him to marry her. She turned the water on full force, trying to wash away the unclean feeling from her body and soul. He was no different from Leonard and Richard . . . and her father. He thought of her as a toy. She didn't know when her tears began mixing with the shower water. All at once harsh sobs were issuing from her mouth into the loofah sponge.

She emerged from the bathroom like a somnambulist, wrapped in an old terry-cloth robe. She would not go through that again, she vowed. How many sessions with the therapist had it taken before she realized that her parents felt threatened by her maturity, by her budding womanhood, so they had punished her as though she were evil. Then Richard and Leonard had used her, taken advantage of her. She raised a fist to her mouth and shook her head. "No, no, no!" Moving like an automaton, she began neatening her apartment.

As soon as she finished straightening up the room, she fell into bed and slept deeply, dreamlessly, not wakening until early afternoon.

Immediately she jumped out of bed and got dressed. She had promised to take the twins to Rockefeller Center to skate. Thank goodness she felt rested after her nap. Eager to do anything that would keep her from thinking of Luc Harrison and the pain she had buried deep inside her, she hurried downstairs to Aileen and David's apartment.

"Are you sure you want to take the twins by yourself?" Aileen asked, covering a yawn.

"I'm sure. You and David go back to bed. I know you were up early with them. Honestly, I feel good, and I'm looking forward to the fresh air and exercise."

"I could call the U.S. Marines and have them give you a hand." Aileen warily eyed her progeny, who were at that moment arguing over the multicolored laces in their skates.

"Don't worry," Misty told her and shepherded her charges out the door.

The twins enjoyed themselves so thoroughly during the bus ride that Misty began to relax and have fun, too.

"Look at that building, Misty," Mary pronounced in awed tones, her nose pressed against the window. "It's all wrapped in ribbon with a big bow." She pointed at the Cartier building on Fifth Avenue.

"I saw that before Christmas when I went with Dad to pick out the tree," Mark announced importantly.

"You're just bragging," Mary accused through pursed lips.

"All right you two, this is our stop," Misty announced, urging them off the bus.

The twins were so excited about skating that they forgot to argue as they walked through Rockefeller Center. It didn't take long for Misty to rent skates for herself. Although she usually found the rentals too tight or too loose, this time they fit comfortably. The twins, who had already put on their own skates, urged her to hurry.

"I am hurrying," she protested. "Mark, I want you to retie yours. You've skipped a few eyelets with the laces."

"Aw, Misty, do I have to?" Mark moaned.

"Yes, you do. It will make skating much more comfortable."

"I didn't miss any of the eyelets with my laces," Mary announced primly, making her brother glower with indignation.

"Let's go, let's go." Misty forestalled an explosion by clasping an arm of each and hurrying them out to the ice.

There were fewer people than she had anticipated. They were probably sleeping late after partying most of the night.

Misty kept an eye on the twins, who were making a rapid if somewhat erratic circle around the rink, and she began to skate herself. She had always been a good skater. As a young girl she had even daydreamed of winning a gold medal in the Olympics. But her father had refused to pay for the expensive coaching that would have been necessary. When she'd begged to earn the money herself by baby-sitting, her parents had told her she was being selfish. Her mother had explained that there were other children in the family who needed more important things, that they couldn't buy luxuries for one child without buying them for all the kids. Misty blessed her aunt and uncle, who had given her not only an old upright piano but also a pair of secondhand skates that she had loved and used for years.

She smiled as she recalled the telephone conversation she had had with her aunt and uncle on Christmas Day. They had urged her to visit them in Florida, and she had made up her mind to do so as soon as she saved enough money for the trip.

Coming out of her reverie, she looked for the twins again and found them in the middle of the rink trying to imitate a young girl about their age who was doing skillful turns and figures. A man and woman skated up to the girl. Then the man lifted his head and looked right at Misty. The smile froze on her face. Luc Harrison! What was he doing here? She looked away from him and continued skating. How was she going to get the twins away? Of course! She would take them to Rumpelmayer's and buy them some ice cream.

But before she could act, she felt her arm being taken in a light but firm grip. She stiffened, and one of her skates caught on an uneven patch of ice.

"Sorry. Did I startle you?" Luc's mouth curved up in a smile, but there was no amusement in his face. His eyes were like icicles that stabbed through her. Tightening his grip on her arm, he kept her moving forward around the ice. The woman he was with remained on his other side toward the center of the rink. "Linda Caseman, this is Mystique Carver. She plays the piano at the Terrace Hotel."

"I've always wanted to be able to play as well as you, but I'm afraid I'm a rank amateur." Linda gave Misty a friendly smile.

Misty smiled back, not sure if the woman was being sarcastic or sincere. Good grief, Luc Harrison had made her paranoid! "It's nice to meet you, but I really have to go," Misty said, trying to pull her arm free.

Luc's grip tightened. "Whose children are they?" he asked, his mouth still smiling but his face tight with tension.

"Aileen and David's . . . my neighbors." Again she tried to jerk her arm free, but she succeeded only in bumping into an older man who was skating by. "Oh! Pardon me."

"No respect—that's the problem today," the senior citizen grumbled, glaring at Misty.

"I think I'll go get a hot chocolate," Linda announced brightly, beginning to skate away from them. "Nice meeting you, Mystique," she called over her shoulder.

"Nice meeting you," Misty mumbled, then dug her fingers into the gloved hand holding her arm. "Will you let me go?" she demanded.

"Stop doing that. You'll knock down someone else." Still Luc didn't release her.

"I didn't knock anyone down," Misty sputtered. "You were the one who— Oh, excuse me." She smiled weakly at the frowning teenager she had just rammed into. "See? You made me do that. Let me go."

"No." Luc put his arm around her waist and began skating faster.

"Stop. I can't skate fast. It makes me dizzy," Misty

argued as the twins' startled faces flashed past her. Finally Luc slowed to a stop. Misty leaned against him, panting. "What . . . in blazes . . . did you think you were . . . doing?" she demanded. "Trying to set a speed-skating record?"

"Tired?" He shot the word at her like a whip.

"No!" She gulped, then whirled away and skated out to the middle of the ice, where Mark and Mary were still trying to master the complicated turns being performed by the young girl Misty had first seen with Luc.

"Hi, Misty," Mary called. "I saw you skating with that man. Janie says he's her uncle. Isn't that funny?"

"Hilarious," Misty said flatly.

"This is Misty." Mark paused in doing figure eights and introduced Janie, who smiled and held out her hand.

Misty admired the young girl's poise. "Hello, Janie."

"Hi. Are you a friend of Uncle Lucas? He said he called a friend today and found out she'd gone skating. Was it you?"

"No," Misty denied. "Ah, what I mean is, I hardly know your uncle. It was very nice meeting you, Janie, but if Mary and Mark want to go to—"

"Rumpelmayer's!" Mary interrupted gleefully. "I want a hot chocolate and a milk shake. Nice meeting you, Janie. Maybe we'll see you again when Misty brings us."

"Yeah," Mark put in, a trace of reserve in his voice as he turned from the girl, and followed Misty and Mary off the ice.

"Mar-rk likes Janie. Mar-rk likes Janie," Mary chanted as they removed their skates.

Misty glimpsed a sheen of angry tears in Mark's eyes. She moved between the twins as she returned her rented skates. "All right, that's enough, Mary," Misty admonished. "If you want to go to Rumpelmayer's, don't say another word."

Mary made a face but fell silent.

Not wanting to catch sight of Luc, Misty kept her eyes on the two youngsters until they were out on the street. She hailed a cab to take them to the ice cream parlor. The sun was shining, but the wind had a cold bite to it. Had Luc called her? Misty wondered. If Aileen had heard the phone and answered it, would she have told Luc that she had gone skating? Misty struggled to keep from thinking of him.

As usual, Rumpelmayer's was a great success with the twins, but somehow the luster of the afternoon was gone for Misty. She had to fight to concentrate on the children who were chattering about their new friend Janie.

That night she shared a supper with David and Aileen after the twins were in bed. "Mary said you know Janie Patterson's uncle," Aileen said, sipping her coffee and watching Misty over the rim of her cup.

"Yes. The girl's uncle is Luc Harrison."

David whistled, then coughed when Aileen glared at him. "He called asking for you," Aileen told Misty.

She shrugged. "The twins loved Rumpelmayer's."

"They always do," Aileen agreed, not protesting Misty's abrupt change of subject. But several times that evening Misty felt her friend's anxious gaze fixed on her, and soon afterward she rose to say good night.

"Just be careful, Misty. Don't get hurt again," Aileen said at the door, hugging her.

"I have no intention of getting hurt," Misty assured her. But her smile wavered.

Because New Year's Day had fallen on a Sunday, the following Monday was a holiday for most people. Not for Misty, however. She was expected at the Edwardian Room at nine that evening.

She was waxing her piano in the morning when she heard the clatter of the twins' feet on the stairs. In the next moment the door flew open and banged against the wall. Mary stood there grinning, Janie smiling shyly at her side. "Look, Misty, isn't it great? Janie came over to take us skating again, and she wants you to come with us."

Misty's gaze flew to the stairs behind the girls, where she expected Luc Harrison to appear at any moment. "I, ah . . . I don't think so. I have to work tonight, and . . . I should practice."

Mary's face fell. "But you *have* to come. Janie wants to go on the bus. She's never gone on the bus before, and you're the only one who knows the way. We can't go without you," Mary wailed.

Janie must have come without her uncle, Misty decided.

She smiled. "All right, I'll come. But remember, I have to be home early so I can take a nap before I go to work." The two girls broke into loud whoops and raced down the stairs.

Misty hurried through the rest of her chores, took a shower, and put on thermal underwear, cord jeans, a blue wool sweater, and a down vest.

When she arrived downstairs, the door to the Collinses' apartment stood open, and she walked in. "All right, slow-pokes, let's move it—" She stopped short, her mouth falling open at the sight of Luc Harrison sitting at Aileen's kitchen table drinking coffee. The three children were already tugging on their coats and boots.

"Isn't this great?" Aileen exclaimed, rushing into nervous speech. "Janie wants to go for a bus ride, and Luc says he'll go, too." She laughed gaily, watching Misty the way a bird watches a snake.

"I see," Misty said calmly, though she wanted to shake her friend. She glared at Luc, who saluted her with his coffee cup, his eyes steady on her, his mouth lifting in a polite smile.

He rose from the table and drained the last of his coffee before putting the cup in the sink. "Very good coffee, Aileen. Thank you. Well, shall we go?" he asked the three young-sters, ignoring Misty's mutinous expression.

The children swept out the door, chattering nonstop. Luc and Misty followed side by side in silence.

Half a block from the bus stop, Misty said, "You had no right to come to the house."

"Janie wanted to skate with Mark and Mary again."

"Then you should have sent her alone. I would have been glad to take her with the twins."

"Thank you so much, but *I* can take care of my niece." Luc's voice was frigid.

"Then do so. But don't include me."

"I won't ever again."

"Good." Misty ran to catch the bus and stepped inside with change in her hand. But another hand pushed past hers and dropped money for all of them into the box. Ignoring that, she made her way to the middle of the bus where Mark, Mary, and Janie were crowded into two seats. Misty tried to sit down next to a plump woman with a big shopping bag on the seat, but the woman glared at her.

"There's an empty seat farther back," the woman muttered, making no effort to move her shopping bag.

"Come along, darling. We'll sit behind the children," Luc said smoothly.

"Yeah, sit behind your kids. Disgusting the way these modern mothers ignore your brats. I never done that," the woman observed to an old man in another seat.

"You're just trying to make trouble," Misty accused Luc.

"*I'm* not the one ignoring our children," he teased mildly.

"They are *not* our children!"

"Mystique, that woman is looking back here again," he whispered. "She probably heard you say that and plans on turning us over to the Society for the Prevention of Cruelty to Children."

"Oh, you . . . you . . ." Misty sputtered.

"What's the matter, Misty?" Mark turned awkwardly around in his seat.

"Nothing, Mark," she said.

"Temper, temper," Luc whispered, a thread of laughter in his voice.

Misty shot a glance at him, surprised by his amusement. Earlier, he had been so furious with her.

Janie turned around, too, and smiled at her. "I like to skate. Do you, Mystique?"

"Her name's Misty," Mary informed her friend. "And she teaches us piano, too."

"Oh? Uncle Luc calls you Mystique, doesn't he?" Janie asked.

"That's the name I use professionally," Misty explained, acutely aware that Luc had draped an arm along the back of the seat.

"I think it's pretty," Janie assured her.

"So do I," Luc murmured.

"We call her Misty," Mark insisted, shooting a suspicious glance at Luc.

When they got off the bus, the three children ran ahead, shouting over their shoulders that they would be careful.

"They have fun together," Luc observed.

"Yes, they do," Misty said, not looking at him.

"Will you have dinner with me this evening?"

"No, thank you. I'm working." Misty was relieved to have an excuse.

"Join me for a meal first," Luc insisted, directing the children across the street.

"I generally don't eat before work. I have a light lunch a few hours before I leave, and that's enough." She clamped her mouth shut, annoyed with herself for having explained it to him.

"You're too thin," Luc observed.

Stung, Misty pulled away from his hold and hurried after the children.

"Stop being so defensive with me," Luc called, catching up with her. "I just meant that I think you should eat more nourishing meals."

"I thought we said everything there was to say to each other yesterday," Misty snapped.

"Yes, we did say quite a bit. I've been wanting to talk to you about that."

"Misty, hurry," Mary wailed. "We want to skate."

"Coming." Misty trotted after them, glad of the diversion as she ushered the children past the kiosk, not bothering to try to pay for them when Luc's hard eyes glinted at her.

She rented a pair of skates and stood on the sideline watching the children as they skated to an open area in the center of the rink and began practicing turns and twists.

"Shall we skate?" Luc took her arm in a firm grip and tugged her out onto the ice. "Don't worry, I have no intention of racing. I just thought you might like to waltz to the Strauss music." His brown eyes held a spark of recklessness that sent a frisson of alarm down Misty's spine.

"I like Strauss's music," she conceded grudgingly.

"Good." Luc spun her around the ice in a gentle waltz. As always, she was caught up in the music. She felt her body and spirit melt into the graceful rhythms of old Vienna.

"You're good," Luc whispered to her, bringing her out of her reverie. "So very, very good. I love the way you move."

"Oh!" Misty tried to look away from his mesmerizing gaze, but she found it too difficult to do so.

They danced close together across the ice for six waltzes.

When they finally slowed to a stop, Misty felt out of breath, partly from the exercise, partly from Luc's lips hovering so close to hers.

"The children," she gasped, pushing away from him. The man was hypnotizing her!

"They're fine," he whispered in her hair.

"See? There they are. Just about where we left them."

"I have to watch them," Misty said, breaking free of his hold and skating to the center of the rink. The children looked up at her and smiled.

"Hi, Misty. Look what I can do," Mary crowed, twirling around with her hands clasped over her head.

From then on, Misty stayed close to the children. Sometimes she skated with one or the other. Once when Luc came close, she went off by herself. Wherever she was on the ice, she was constantly aware of his piercing gaze.

When it was time to go, both Mark and Mary held back. "Aw, Misty, just a little while longer," Mary begged.

"Come on, Misty," Mark wheedled.

"It's nice today. Not as crowded as other days," Janie offered.

Misty hesitated, wanting to please the children but knowing that if she didn't leave now she wouldn't have time for a nap before she had to go to work. Luc took the decision out of her hands.

"Everybody off with the skates," he commanded, sending the twins and Janie scurrying to the sidelines.

Misty stared after them, amazed to see that they appeared neither angry nor sullen. She glanced up at Luc. "Thank you. I should get home."

"But you would have given in to them," Luc said softly, a flicker of warmth in his brown eyes.

Misty shrugged. "I suppose so."

"You need someone to take care of you."

She stiffened; her temper flared. "No, thank you," she said coolly. "I take care of myself." She skated away, her back ramrod straight.

As they rode home on the bus, Luc and Misty sat close together but didn't speak. Misty was content to listen to the children's chatter. Gradually her ire settled into a renewed resolve not to get caught in any man's trap ever again.

Luc walked with them to the house, saw them inside, and left with his niece, his quiet nod toward Misty in marked contrast to the children's noisy good-byes.

Misty didn't stay long either, although she could tell Aileen was dying to ask her about the afternoon she had spent with Luc Harrison. "I really do have to get some sleep, so I'll pass on the offer of coffee," she told her disappointed friend.

Misty went up to her own apartment, deliberately erasing Luc Harrison from her thoughts. After packing the carrier with makeup and accessories, she climbed into the water bed, curled into a ball, and willed herself to go to sleep.

In the end she overslept and had to race through the apartment, making her bed, showering, and pulling on a pair of pale green velvet jeans and a matching chamois vest. Her emerald green blouse was almost the same color as her eyes. She wore tiny earrings that she would later exchange for dangling gold ones to complement her persimmon-colored silk dress.

She took the elevator downstairs, her purse and carrier bumping against her legs.

"Good night, Misty. Take care," Dave called out from the doorway of his apartment. "Why don't you hail a taxi instead of taking all that stuff on the bus?"

"I'm fine," she assured him, closing the heavy oak door behind her and hurrying down the stoop. Since she could afford a taxi only once a day, she saved it for coming home.

She had reached the sidewalk and was hitching the carrier higher on her shoulder when a familiar voice said, "I'll take that for you." She turned, aghast. Luc was standing beside her, removing the carrier from her shoulder and stuffing it into the trunk of a bronze-colored Ferrari parked at the curb.

Her mouth agape, Misty made no move to protest when he opened the passenger door and ushered her inside. "Where did you come from?" she demanded. "I didn't see you when I came out the door." She sank back against the soft leather upholstery; she knew she should get out of the car but for some reason she was unable to do so.

"You were too busy wrestling with that carrier. Do you take the bus to work every night?"

"I don't work every night." Feeling his gaze on her,

Misty kept her eyes focused straight ahead.

"You're a proud little thing."

"I don't know why you keep coming around. We said everything there was to say yesterday morning."

"Not quite," he disagreed, firing the powerful engine and pulling smoothly into heavy traffic.

"But why do you keep coming?" she repeated, confused. "I won't change my mind."

"I know. I've changed mine."

"About what?"

He didn't answer. Instead he concentrated on maneuvering the sleek car through the congested traffic. Misty gazed distractedly out the window at the people hurrying along the sidewalks. Where were they going? Home? Out to dinner? To a show?

Finally Luc drew the car up outside the Terrace Hotel. As Misty began fumbling with the door handle he said mildly, "Don't bother, darling. It's locked on the wheel." He parked and turned to her. "I've thought over what you told me yesterday, and I realize your request has merit." He pressed a button on the steering wheel, and the door on her side of the car unlocked. Then he got out, removed her things from the trunk, and ushered her up the steps to the entrance.

"What do you mean?" Misty asked as a thin thread of panic uncurled inside her.

"Shall I park your car, sir?" the parking attendant asked Luc.

"No, thank you," Luc replied. He walked with Misty into the lobby, handed her the carrier, kissed her on the cheek, and left without explaining how he'd changed his mind.

Misty stood staring after him, thoroughly perplexed. But in another moment she realized it was time to change and she hurried to her dressing room. Once dressed, she studied herself in the mirror. Morey had been right again. For some reason the persimmon-colored gown seemed to enhance her hair rather than clash with it. She applied pale gold eye shadow—tonight she would have cat's eyes—and leaned closer to the mirror. Was the gown cut a shade too low in front?

The crisp silk was molded tightly to her bosom and clung as though magnetized to her form. The wide neckline skimmed her shoulders, and the long sleeves ended tightly above her wrists. There was no extra material to get in her way as she played the piano. The dress was light and very comfortable, and it gave the skin on her neck and above her breasts a peachy pearlescence. Misty laughed with delight at her image as she put on dangling gold earrings, her only jewelry except for a thin gold watch. She found costume jewelry a distraction when she played and rarely wore it.

Misty strolled out of the dressing room twenty minutes early and went over to Willis, who was gesturing to her. "Hi. How's the crowd in the Edwardian Room?" she asked.

"We're full up, as we've been since you began playing here," Willis told her. "Here. You have time to eat some soup and bread and drink a glass of milk. I've put it all out for you on the little table behind the palm tree."

Misty blinked at him in surprise. "Willis, you know I never eat before I play."

"But this won't be a lot of food. Come on and sit down." He ushered her to a chair at the small corner table and gestured to one of the waiters.

"I don't think I should do this," she protested faintly, tantalized in spite of herself by the fragrant soup.

"Eat," Willis commanded.

She did. The clear beef broth with vegetables tasted great with the French crackers, while the glass of milk was a welcome addition. "Thank you, Willis. That was delicious. I do feel better." Misty put her hand on the maître d's sleeve.

"It's about time I fed you. I don't know why I didn't think of it before," he grumbled, then turned away to speak to a portly man in a cashmere suit.

Misty wanted to ask Willis what he meant, but he was busy and, besides, it was time to begin playing.

Her sense of well-being affected her playing in a positive manner. She found herself straying from her usual repertoire of popular songs and show tunes to play a rousing piece by Nicolai Rimsky-Korsakov. She smiled at the audience's burst of applause, then moved immediately into Rachmaninoff, chuckling when she heard a collective sigh rise from some of the diners. She returned to her standard repertoire feeling refreshed.

The evening passed quickly. At midnight she realized she felt less fatigued than usual. She looked up to smile at her audience . . . and gazed right into Luc Harrison's brown eyes. He raised his glass to her and tipped some of the brown liquid into his mouth. She caught her breath as a tingling warmth started in her toes and worked its way upward.

After that, she couldn't seem to control her eyes. They strayed at will toward Luc. Each time, she found him watching her. Adrenaline rushed through her veins. Her fingers seemed to take on a life of their own as they skimmed skillfully over the piano keys. A few stragglers lingered in the dining room and applauded loudly after each song as she continued to play, putting all her heart and soul into the music.

Finally there was no one left but Luc. In accordance with house rules, she could have quit for the night, but she didn't. Instead, she continued to play ever more difficult pieces.

At two-thirty a hand came down over hers on the keyboard. "That's enough, darling. You're tired."

Misty nodded, staring mesmerized at Luc as his determined gaze kindled a warmth in her such as she had never felt before. "I think I could play all night," she whispered to him.

"I know," he told her, lifting her from the piano bench and slipping an arm around her. "Go and change. I'll drive you home tonight."

"Isn't this awfully late for you? Don't you have to work at the bank in the morning?"

"Yes to both questions. But I think I may have a solution to the problem."

"Oh?"

"Never mind that now. I'll tell you later." He led her to the wide corridor and patted her backside. "Go and change."

"I . . . I . . ." Misty stood, irresolute.

"Stop thinking up excuses, Mystique. I'll just have to refute them."

She turned away, frowning as she said good night to Willis and went into her dressing room. After scrubbing the makeup off her face, she changed into the velvet jeans and emerald green blouse she'd worn on her way over to the hotel. I don't understand him, she thought. He confuses me. Tonight I'm going to tell him again that I want nothing to do with him. She stifled the ache that the words brought deep inside. If she was to survive, she had to keep men like Luc Harrison out of her life. It was the only way. She left the dressing room, wearing no makeup except a little lip gloss.

Luc was waiting for her. He took the carrier out of her hands. "You look twelve years old," he said, staring at her.

"I'm not."

"I'm glad," he said, imitating her stern tone. But his eyes glinted with amusement.

"Mr. Harrison..." she began as they walked out the front door to the Ferrari. Louis, the parking attendant, was holding open the passenger door. "Thank you, Louis." She tried to smile.

Luc got in, started the car, and pulled away from the curb. "Put your head back and rest," he told her. "You can say anything you want when we get home."

Misty turned in the seat to face him. "I want to tell you now, Mr. Harrison.

"Luc."

"All right, Luc. I want to tell you—"

"Put your head back and relax, love. Then you can talk to me."

Misty settled back, her eyes skimming the facades of the buildings they passed and the darkened interior of the car. "You keep interrupting me," she complained.

He laughed lightly. "I promise not to do it anymore," he said, pressing his hand on her knee for just a second, seeming not to notice when she quivered at his touch.

"Good," she said, suddenly hoarse. "Luc, I want you to stop coming to the Terrace Hotel."

"Darling, how can I? I'm one of the owners."

"You're doing it again," Misty said, rolling her head to stare at him.

"Sorry, sweet."

"We talked this through on New Year's Day, in your apartment."

"My suite in the hotel," he corrected her.

"Stop interrupting!"

"All right," he whispered.

"Luc!"

"I'm listening."

"We talked, and we decided we wouldn't see each other again."

"Now I *have* to interrupt," he said, trying to soothe her with a squeeze on her knee that made her jump. "I did not agree that we shouldn't see each other again. I admit that I was a little thrown by your demands, but I did not say that I wouldn't see you again."

"Well, now you can," Misty declared.

He shook his head. "I can't do that. Primarily because it would be a lie." He turned the car onto the entrance ramp leading to a small underground garage where only two other cars were parked.

With a start of surprise Misty sat up abruptly, looking around her. "Where are we?" she demanded.

"Now, don't panic. We're in the underground garage I share with three other brownstone owners in the neighborhood. Although the cost is outrageous—"

"I don't want to hear how expensive it is to park your Ferrari." Her voice rose to a shriek. "Take me home."

Luc parked the car, removed the keys, and got out. He went around to her side, opened the door, and leaned in to take her arm. She shrank back, cringing. Luc's mouth tightened ominously. "Darling, don't ever flinch from me." He went down on his haunches so that they were eye to eye and lifted her hand to his mouth, his eyes never leaving her face. "Please come in for a moment, Mystique. I want to show you something." He pulled an envelope from his pocket.

"I want to go home. It's late." She swallowed, her throat dry.

"Just let me show you these papers." He glanced around the garage. "This place is well lit, but not for reading. Besides, I want to show you something else."

Reluctantly she swung her legs around and let Luc help her to her feet. "I won't stay long."

"It won't take you more than fifteen minutes to read these papers," Luc assured her, leading her to a doorway with a steel nameplate that read: Lucas S. Harrison. "This stairway leads to the basement of my brownstone," he explained. "Above us are the owners' four backyards. Each one is separated by trees and fencing to ensure a measure of privacy for all the tenants." He led her up cement steps, his hand enveloping hers. At the top he unlocked another steel door and switched on a light. "This is the wine cellar. It feels cool, doesn't it? Through here, Mystique." He ushered her down a wide pathway with wine bottles on either side to a thick oak door, which he also opened. It led onto a more spacious area of the basement. "I keep gym equipment down here." He gestured toward a weight machine, a punching bag, and a padded exercise board.

"Nice," Misty murmured, glancing at the unfinished brick walls.

"If you'd like an exercycle, we can get that, too," he said.

Misty stared at him. "I don't care what you put in here. I swim at an athletic club three times a week."

Luc considered the room. "I don't think we could fit a pool in here, darling."

"I'm not your darling," she snapped, preceding him up a wide staircase that led into what Misty surmised to be the front foyer of the house.

"That's the front door leading to the street," Luc confirmed, pointing to an oak door inset with a stained-glass window. "We'll go into the living room. On the second floor is my library, on the third floor is the master suite, and on the fourth floor are three more bedrooms. There are four bathrooms. Down here, besides the living and dining rooms, is the kitchen and a larger room that I use for entertaining. I have day help, but no live-in—"

Just then Misty heard a rhythmic clicking coming across the oak floor. A large brown Doberman stuck his head around an open door. Misty stepped back, paralyzed with fright. A thousand remembered nightmares filled her thoughts, foremost among them the image of the dog that had bitten her when she was thirteen. The growling, snapping, and snarling seemed to be all around her, as fresh in her mind as the moment the animal had attacked her, leaping out at her as she walked past his house. Later, when the owner had suggested to her father that she had provoked the dog, her father had agreed without hesitation that she probably had.

"Darling, for God's sake!" Luc exclaimed. "Are you afraid of dogs?" He took her into his arms, cradling her, protecting her, trying to lift her chin, which she burrowed against his chest. "Bruno, down," he ordered. "Good boy."

Misty took several deep breaths. "A dog like that bit me," she said shakily. "It wasn't my fault."

"No, of course it wasn't. You're trembling." Luc tipped up her chin. "Don't be afraid."

Gradually, feeling warm in Luc's embrace, she grew calm. She turned her head to study the dog, who was lying on the floor, his head between his paws, whining softly. Misty gave a weak laugh. "He thinks I'm crazy, doesn't he?"

"I think he's worried about you. I found him on a country road when he was just a pup. He's been with me ever since. He's gentle and very intelligent."

"Yes," Misty agreed, though she still wasn't sure of the animal.

"I'll send him into the kitchen."

"Should I introduce myself?" She gasped at her own boldness, afraid yet wanting to rid herself of the fear.

"It might help," Luc agreed. "I'll hold you. Don't worry. Bruno, come." The Doberman rose in one fluid motion and stepped toward them, stopping inches away from Misty. She closed her eyes. Fear turned her legs to jelly. "Open your eyes, darling, and say hello," Luc whispered.

She opened one eye. "Hello, Bruno."

The dog wagged his stub of a tail.

"That's enough for the first lesson, I think." Luc ordered the dog to the kitchen and led her into a huge room with a fireplace and walls paneled in hand-carved oak. "Sit here." Luc gestured toward a couch that matched the green in the Persian carpet. He sank down near her feet and put a lit match to the kindling in the fireplace, then turned and handed her the papers he'd shown her in the garage. "Here's what I want you to read."

Misty tried to smile. "Why don't you just tell me what they say."

He rose from the floor to sit close beside her. "All right." He put the papers in his lap, lifting the first one. "This is my bank statement certified by my board of directors and accountants. With it is a list of my tangible assets and liabilities. I'm a rich man, Mystique."

"That has nothing to do with me," she said in a faint voice, staring from the papers to his face and back again.

"Shhh. You mustn't interrupt me. There, you can peruse my financial statements at your leisure, and of course you are free to ask further questions and get any additional proof you might want."

"Proof?" she repeated.

He lifted the second paper. "This is a statement from my personal physician with a copy of all tests that I've had in the last three years. I'm very healthy and, as you specified, free of disease."

"Lord . . ." Misty groaned.

"Shhh. You can look at all the X-rays and tests I've had, and of course you can question my doctor."

She shook her head, unable to say anything. A terrible dread had settled over her. She could almost guess what was coming next.

"This last paper is our marriage license, which is valid as of today. Since I see no reason to wait, I've arranged for us to be married tomorrow afternoon, upstate in the town of Hudson. I managed to get your blood test waived, so we're all set."

Misty sagged against the back of the couch, staring in shocked speechlessness at the man beside her.

CHAPTER FOUR

MISTY SURGED TO her feet. "I have to go home." If need be, she'd run to Alaska to get away from Luc Harrison.

"You're tired, darling. Why don't you sleep here tonight? Then we'll have a leisurely drive up to Hudson tomorrow." He stood up, clasping her lightly to his side.

"I can't marry you," Misty said with a gasp.

From Luc's expression she could tell he felt affronted. "I won't accept that," he said firmly. "I fulfilled all your specifications. There is no insanity in the family—well, no *overt* insanity. I have a few strange relatives, but what family doesn't?"

"You don't know me," Misty protested.

"I *do* know you. The day I first saw you playing the piano in the Edwardian Room I hired a private investigator to learn all about you."

"You what!" She was shocked. "Checking to see if I was a social pariah, I suppose," she said with deadly sarcasm.

"No. Checking to see if you had a husband I would have to take care of."

"What would you have done? Bought him off? Killed him?"

"Yes," Luc said promptly.

Misty stared at him. Her mouth had gone dry. "I won't marry anybody who's investigated me like the FBI."

"Why not? You're free to investigate me. I've never been married, though I've had a mistress or two."

"Or forty," Misty shot back with scathing anger, feeling less and less numb as she began to recover from the initial shock.

"All right, I shouldn't have had you investigated. But I had to know all about you. I couldn't wait to court you and ask you questions about your marital status. I was in a hurry. You *are* going to marry me."

"You don't know anything about me. I . . . I've had my share of problems. I'm not the kind of woman who will fit in with your family." She had no intention of telling him that her father had once accused her of being a whore.

"Then we won't see my family," Luc assured her. "I'm fond of them, but I don't see them all the time. Of course I'll want you to meet my father and mother." Luc smiled down at her. "Father thinks you're beautiful. He told me my mother's hair was just a shade lighter than yours when they were first married, but my mother says her hair was more blond."

"Your parents know who I am?"

"Yes, but they'll really get to know you after we're married. I took them to hear you play at the hotel, and they were very impressed, as I knew they would be. You play so well."

"Luc, you didn't . . . I didn't see them with you," Misty babbled.

"We were sitting at a corner table out of your line of vision." He opened the double doors of the living room and led her out to the foyer. "Shall we say good night to Bruno?"

"If you have to walk him, I'll wait here," Misty said, her mind awhirl.

"You're thinking that you'll run out the door and go home while I'm walking the dog. But I'm not about to let you roam the streets of Manhattan at this time of night. Besides, I would come after you and take you up to Hudson to get married anyway."

"We aren't in love."

He shrugged. "Define *love* for me. I know I want to marry you. I know you told me you wanted no other type of relationship with a man. So, I'm all set." He looked down at her, determination showing in his rigid stance and hard jaw.

Misty was at a loss for words. She felt as if she'd been swept up in a strong current and washed helplessly downstream.

"Didn't you tell me that you wanted marriage?" Luc queried.

"I said I wouldn't have any other type of relationship, but . . . but I didn't—"

"I'm holding you to that, Mystique."

"Misty. Everyone calls me Misty," she declared, losing her patience.

"Except your husband-to-be."

"We can't get married. People like us don't get married. They live together until they're sure, and then . . . then . . ."

"You don't want that, and I've found that I don't want it either. You can sleep alone tonight if you wish, but no matter what you decide, I want two things from you now."

"What?" Her voice had a hollow ring.

"I don't want you to try to leave this house alone, and I want you to promise that you won't go back on our agreement."

"What agreement? I didn't make any—"

"We're just going around and around in circles, love. You're tired. We'll talk in the morning. Come on, I'll show you our room. You can sleep there tonight. I'll sleep upstairs."

"This is crazy, this is crazy," Misty kept whispering to herself all the way up the stairs.

She was too distraught to appreciate the beautiful beige and cream-colored bedroom with the huge bed in the center. "I have a water bed," she said inanely.

"We'll toss this one out and get a water bed," Luc offered.

"I have to have my piano. It costs a great deal to move a concert grand," she informed him as he unzipped her jeans.

"I know. I had three Steinways moved in here two weeks ago. They're all in perfect tune, so you should have no trouble."

"*Three* Steinways? That's disgusting," she told him, her voice going hoarse. Without thinking, she stepped out of her jeans.

"Would you like to sleep in the buff, sweets, or do you want the top of my pajamas?"

"I sleep in a flannel nightgown, and sometimes in flannel pajamas," she babbled.

"With feet in them, I'll bet."

"I used to until we were able to buy a better heating system for the house," Misty told him blankly. "This is a dream." Her voice was muffled as he slipped his silk pajama top over her head. "What will you wear now that I have your pajamas?" She looked down at herself, noting that the hem of the top fell below her knees.

"My mother buys them for me so that if the place burns down I won't have to run naked into the street. She has high hopes that I'll at least keep them at my bedside."

"You sleep in the nude," Misty pronounced solemnly.

"Yes. You'll get used to it."

"I am signing myself into an asylum tomorrow," she told him, wiping at the tears on her cheeks.

"I'll make you happy," he promised.

"You'll hate me in three months," she vowed.

"Never." Luc led her to the bed and stared down at her with an expression that sent warmth to all her extremities and set off a throbbing pulse in her very core. After a few moments he urged her under the sheets. "Would you like some company to keep you warm?" he asked, his voice sounding thick to Misty, who was half asleep.

"No." She yawned. "I always sleep alone. You go walk the dog."

"After tomorrow you won't sleep alone," he muttered, his voice growing fainter as Misty sank deeper into sleep.

The sound of an insistent buzzing almost awakened her. Then the noise stopped, and she snuggled into the warm down quilt that covered her, rolling over onto her stomach.

"Wake up, darling." Luc shook her gently, chuckling

when she groaned as he pulled the quilt off the bed. "I fully intended to let you sleep longer, but we have a problem that—Lord, where did you get those scars on your back-side?" He cursed softly as he lifted the pajama top higher and examined her. "If you hadn't twisted the top up, I might not have noticed these. I sure as hell didn't notice them when I undressed you." He muttered another low curse as his hand gently traced the raised welts.

Misty shivered and, pushing the pillow off her head, turned on her side to face him, trying in vain to pull the pajama top down. "Give me back the covers," she mumbled, regarding him through bleary eyes.

Luc didn't bother to remove the towel from around his waist before he slipped into bed beside her and gathered her close to him. "Tell me. Was that where the dog bit you, darling?"

Misty nodded, burrowing her face into his neck and reveling in his warmth. "I hadn't teased the dog. I was just walking past on the sidewalk."

"And your father accused you of teasing the animal," Luc said in low tones.

"Yes." She gulped. "He and Mr. Marris, the owner of the dog, said that I must have provoked it because Sandy was usually friendly." The words bubbled from her like air escaping from a balloon.

"Why didn't the doctor recommend cosmetic surgery?"

"My father didn't take me to the doctor until the bites were infected."

"Damn him! You might have contracted tetanus from being left untreated." Luc cuddled her closer.

"My mother poured iodine on the bites." Misty shivered as she remembered how much it had hurt. She'd screamed so loudly.

"Good God," Luc whispered, his hand trembling as he stroked her hair.

They lay there in silence, Luc's slow hand soothing her. Then, abruptly, he stiffened. "I forgot. I got a call from Aileen. It seems we have visitors. Your three sisters have come to stay with you."

"My sisters?" Misty shot up to a sitting position in bed and whirled to face him as he rolled onto his back, his hands clasped behind his head. "Are you sure? My sisters?"

He nodded.

Misty bit her lip. "I haven't seen them in years. Gosh, they must be——"

"Eighteen, nineteen, and twenty-one," Luc supplied. He reached up and twisted a finger in her thick hair. "Don't worry. I called my sister Alice, and she's going right over to your apartment. She has three grown children, two boys and a girl, all of whom are living on their own in various parts of the country. She and her husband John love their family and miss them. When I told her she might get the chance to have young boarders, she was ecstatic."

"They came to *me,*" Misty said in wonder. "They need *me.* I have to go to them." She jumped out of bed, jerking the pajama top down over her backside when she heard Luc suck in his breath.

"Okay, darling. If you want them to live with us, that's fine with me. We have plenty of room. But this morning we'll explain that it's our wedding day and arrange to have them stay with Alice and John."

"Surely you don't mean to go through with this charade," Misty protested.

His face grew taut. "We *are* getting married."

"Today?" Misty asked weakly.

Luc rose from the bed. The towel had slipped, and she averted her gaze. "As much as I would like to dally with you in this bed, I think we'd better get dressed. You'll find clean underwear in the left cupboard in the dressing room. I indulged myself one day in Saks. I enjoy shopping for you. See if you like my choices. I'll use the other bathroom on this floor." He padded out of the bedroom, leaving Misty still sputtering.

Without thinking, she went automatically into the dressing room and pulled open the door he had indicated. "Buy me underthings," she fumed, fingering the silky, peach-colored briefs and bra, as she slipped into them. She pulled on her velvet jeans and now wrinkled blouse and ran a comb through her long curly red hair, then ran out of the bedroom and down the curving staircase to the foyer, looking for Luc.

"Out here, darling," he called to her from under the stairs. "Come and sit down."

"We have to hurry," she whispered, smiling politely at a heavy-set woman whose plump face was wreathed in smiles. She glanced warily at the Doberman, who cocked his head at her.

At once, Luc was at her side, leading her past the dog to a chair in the dining room, where he seated her. "I know, love. I just want you to have some freshly squeezed orange juice and—here you are. A vitamin pill and one toasted English muffin. Mrs. Wheaton makes them herself."

"How do you do, Mrs. Wheaton?" Misty could feel her smile trembling as the dog rose and ambled over to her side.

"How do you do, miss?" Mrs. Wheaton greeted her. "May I offer you my best wishes?"

"Ah, thank you." Misty turned to glare at Luc as he picked up her vitamin pill and gestured for her to open her mouth. Snatching it out of his hand, she popped it into her mouth and swallowed. His kiss of approval emboldened her to risk patting Bruno's sleek brown head.

After they had finished eating breakfast, Misty urged Luc down the stairs to the garage. In the car he glanced at her pinched face and, loosening her clenched fingers, clasped his right hand around her left one. "Stop worrying," he scolded. "Everything will be fine. You're not to worry ever again."

"But I want my sisters to be all right."

"I will personally see to it that everything is just the way you want it, darling," he promised. "But nothing is going to interfere with our marriage at four o'clock today."

Misty didn't respond. Images of impending doom sprung up in her mind. By the time Luc parked the car in front of her brownstone, she was trembling, and her teeth were chattering.

Luc helped her out of the car, his arm tight around her, her carrier slung over his other shoulder. "Take it easy, love," he soothed.

As they walked up the stoop, the front door was flung open, and Mary stood bright-eyed on the threshold. "They're in our house, and I'm going to take Betsy skating, and Marcy wants to see the New York Public Library, and Celia is pretty," she exclaimed all in one breath, beaming at Luc and Misty. "Oh, and another lady is here, and she's nice, too." Mary chattered nonstop all the way down the hall to the door of her apartment.

As Misty walked in, her eyes alighted immediately on her sisters. She opened her arms, and the three young women ran into them.

Celia, Betsy, and Marcy cried. Misty felt raw pain, but her eyes remained dry.

"We made up our minds to come a long time ago, Misty," said chestnut-haired Celia, wiping her tears away. "But we couldn't leave Betsy behind, so we waited until she was eighteen. It wasn't as bad for us, but Father was getting worse, especially with Marcy when she said she wanted to go to college."

"I'm so glad you came to me," Misty said, her voice husky. "I've missed you." All at once she felt guilty. Why had she always assumed that her sisters would be spared the parental coldness and censure she had suffered once she began to mature? She had always been so certain that some flaw in herself had caused the gap between her and her parents. Despite the progress she'd made in therapy, she had never quite shaken that feeling.

"I was afraid you might not want us," Betsy said, her voice trembling.

"Of course we want you," Luc said, stepping forward and introducing himself. "You will always have a home with Mystique and me."

Misty heard Aileen gasp, but her attention was diverted as an unfamiliar woman came forward, her hand outstretched. "Hello, Mystique, I'm Luc's sister Alice Hemings. Luc has told me all about you. I'm so pleased to hear you're getting married today." Aileen, Mark, and Mary all gasped at this piece of information. "I would so love to have your sisters come and stay with me until you and Luc return from your honeymoon."

After that, pandemonium broke loose. The babble of voices filled the room as everybody but Misty spoke at once, firing questions, shouting congratulations, expressing surprise. Misty felt cut loose, disoriented, unable to respond.

Finally Luc succeeded in getting across the message that he and Misty wouldn't be going on a honeymoon right away and that they would be back in a few days.

"Well, not too soon, I hope," said Alice. "I want the girls to have some fun—go riding, shopping, sight-seeing." She ticked off the activities on her fingers.

Mark stared open-mouthed as Alice explained to him that her family owned horses and that he was welcome to come out to Heath Farms at any time to ride. Both he and Mary gazed at Alice with saucer-eyed delight.

After a while Misty and her sisters excused themselves and went upstairs to Misty's apartment for some private conversation. "We couldn't stay any longer," Celia said. "We thought about it a long time. He was so smothering, so critical."

"He wasn't always like that," Misty interjected softly, knowing that it was true, also fully aware that she couldn't have made such a statement a few months ago. "When I was small, they were both good to me."

"But they changed as we grew older," Marcy mused. "One by one we all felt the change."

Her sisters nodded.

"Why did they even have children?" Betsy asked, her voice anguished.

"I don't know, Bets, but I do know you'll be happy here," Misty promised, her heart aching for her sisters. Why had she never suspected that the girls were going through the same painful experience she had endured?

"Don't look like that, Misty," Marcy pleaded. "We didn't have it as bad as you did. Honest." Marcy's glasses glinted in the light coming through the wall of windows. "He was never after us like he was after you. But he was getting worse, and Mom never seemed to care about anything as long as she could do as she liked."

"They hated watching us become independent," Betsy said with sudden insight.

Awhile later Luc knocked and entered the room. "Darling, I hate to rush you, but it's time for you to get dressed. Alice wants to take your sisters to Saks to do a little shopping before driving to Long Island." He chuckled as Misty's sisters whooped with joy.

"Imagine us shopping in Saks," Betsy said dreamily after Luc had left. "By the way, Misty, I think Luc is terrific. I hope I find a husband just like him."

"Me, too." Marcy pushed her glasses back up her nose and grinned at Misty. "It's so good to be here."

"I should stay with you," Misty said, feeling as though she were caught in a whirlwind. Both pain and joy assailed her at the thought of becoming Luc's wife. She realized she wanted to marry him! The mere thought was like sliding off the top of a mountain into wonderland!

"No, don't stay with us," the girls chorused.

"Marry Luc. It will make us happy to see you happy," Marcy added. "I think you should have a nice quiet ceremony with just the two of you—even though I *would* like to be there."

"We can have a party when you come back," Celia suggested.

"You don't mind staying with Luc's sister?" Misty asked, aware that she had accepted the idea of marrying Luc that day. Still, she couldn't seem to get off the emotional roller coaster she'd been riding since she'd met him at Christmastime.

"Alice is nice," Marcy went on. "As soon as she arrived, she told us she would be delighted to have us come and stay with her." Marcy smiled. "Besides, you'll be back soon."

Celia and Betsy added their agreement.

Later, her sisters returned downstairs while Misty went through her closet, trying to decide what to wear. She wanted to talk herself out of marrying Luc, but she couldn't summon the will to do so. Gradually she was fully accepting that she would be his wife. "Damn the consequences," she muttered. "I'll handle them as they come." She was staring into her closet when someone knocked on the door. "Come in," she called. She turned in surprise as Morey and Zena walked in.

"Get away from those mundane clothes and look at what you're going to wear," Morey told her.

"Whoever would have thought you'd get married before me," Zena said. "And he's so nice."

"How do you know?" Misty had one eye on her friend

and one eye on the cream-colored silk suit Morey was pulling from a garment bag.

"He called and offered to let us use your apartment,"
Zena explained, biting her lip. "I realize now we should
have asked you first."

"Oh, no," Misty said, hugging first Zena, then Morey.
"You'd make me so happy by moving in here. Can you
imagine how good it would be for Aileen, David, and the
children? Oh, please, please, live here."

"We will. Now never mind that business," Morey said,
separating the two women and urging Misty out of her
clothes so she could try on the suit. "Let's hope Superman
doesn't come through the door when you're standing in your
undies. He's liable to blacken my eyes."

"Don't be silly," Misty scoffed.

"That's all right, Morey. I'm here to protect you," Zena
assured him.

"I may blacken his eyes anyway," Luc said from the
doorway. Misty whirled around. Luc's eyes pinned her to
the spot, heating her flesh with their burning intensity.

Zena jumped up and hurried over to Luc, reaching up
to cover his eyes. "You can't see her in her wedding outfit.
It would be bad luck." She ushered him out the door.

It didn't take Morey long to complete the small adjust-
ments needed. Misty pulled out of her closet a pair of cream
satin pumps that went perfectly with the suit.

When she finally descended the stairs on Morey's arm,
she wore an ivory comb in her hair and carried a tussie-
mussie, an old-fashioned bouquet of cream-colored tea roses
that Luc had bought her.

He was waiting at the foot of the stairs. As she reached
the final step, he came forward to take her hand and stood
silent while her friends and sisters all talked at once.

"I don't think even Saks could upstage this moment,"
Alice said as she kissed Misty's cheek. "How beautiful you
are. Thanks for letting me take care of your sisters. My
house is just crying for them." She lowered her voice. "Be
happy. I think you're just what the doctor ordered. Luc's
cynicism had begun to run too deep. Love will change that."

Misty looked blankly at Alice. "I don't understand."

"Never mind. You'll find out." Luc gave his sister an

irritated glance, but Alice just grinned.

"Come on, darling," he told Misty. "We have to hurry. Good-bye everyone." He placed a fox fur jacket around her shoulders, and she felt his strong arm propel her out of the house.

"But I don't wear furs," she protested. "I don't believe in killing animals." Despite her words, she couldn't help noticing how warm the coat was as she stepped into the cold wind whistling down the street.

"I should have known." Luc chuckled and kissed her cheek as he held open the car door before walking around to climb under the wheel. He tooted the horn and they both waved to the people huddled on the stoop as he pulled the car into traffic. "I won't make that mistake again, love," he promised. "But indulge me this time, won't you? I don't want you to catch cold."

"Thank you," Misty said. "It really is lovely. I don't want to sound ungrateful."

"You don't. You sound like a woman who doesn't like to see animals killed for their skins. You're sweet."

Misty drew in a deep breath. "I can't believe we're really going to get married. It's crazy."

"Maybe, but we're going to do it."

"Luc, will you admit that we don't have much in common, that all things that should be in a good marriage— knowing one another well, love—"

"Forget it, Misty. We're getting married at four o'clock today, and our marriage will be a good one." Misty let her head fall back against the cushioned seat. Neither one of them spoke for several long moments. Finally Luc said, "Don't worry about your sisters. Alice is the kindest person I know, and her husband is an old softie. I intend to make sure your sisters have happy lives from now on."

"Luc, thank you."

"We'll be happy, Mystique." He reached over and clasped her hand warmly. She looked with amazement at their entwined fingers.

"Will we be coming back today?" she asked.

"No. I've made reservations in an old country inn where I used to stay when I went skiing upstate."

"Oh."

"I think you'll like it."

"I don't ski," she mumbled, feeling like Alice falling into a deep, deep rabbit hole into Wonderland.

"I'll teach you, darling. Not that I plan on doing much skiing during the short time we'll be there." He chuckled, then shot her an annoyed glance. "Don't scrunch up to the window like that, Mystique. Nothing bad is going to happen to you."

"You don't know me."

"I've already told you I know everything I need to know about—"

"But you don't know what I'm like deep inside. And I still resent your having investigated me."

"I know. I'm going to try to change. It won't happen right away or all at once, but I want to be the kind of husband you can be proud of." Luc paused before adding, "I overheard what Alice said to you about my cynicism." He sighed and reached out to squeeze her thigh. "I am . . . I *was* a cynic about almost everything, but especially about women. But in the short time we've known each other, my feelings have changed. I'm not the same man I used to be. I want to be a man you can be proud of," he repeated.

"Please, Luc, don't say that. I don't want you to change for me . . . or do anything for me." Misty fought to keep the stridency from her voice.

"Calm down, love. Everything will be fine."

Misty was about to argue with him, but it was so much easier to lie back and watch the countryside roll past the window. Luc snapped a tape into the player, and soft piano music filled the car. Misty recognized the skill of the musician who was playing and listened carefully, taking note of his careful phrasing and meticulous technique. As she absorbed the music, her gaze ran desultorily over the landscape through which they were traveling. The thrumming of the music, the rich purr of the engine, and the pulsing rhythm of the piano were like narcotics to Misty. Gradually she fell asleep.

She began to dream. Her father appeared, making her shift restlessly, though she didn't waken. Lord, she didn't want to remember. But she couldn't help it. Suddenly she was sixteen again.

"No, Father, I didn't do anything wrong. I didn't," Misty pleaded, her stomach churning with anguish.

"Slut! You're pregnant with Howie Breston's kid. Even his parents know about it!" Misty's father shook his fist in her face. "I never laid a hand on you, but I'm sorry now. Whore!" He turned to his wife, who was standing next to him, wringing her hands. "See! See what your daughter is, Marilyn? A whore."

"Alvan, don't use that coarse word in front of me."

"But, my dear, you can see what she is." He turned back to Misty. "Look at her. Her lips are blue, and she's shaking. She hates to hear the truth about herself. She's a stupid slut."

"I'm not, I'm not," Misty whispered, nausea rising inside her. "Howie wouldn't say that about me. It's not true. I never let him . . . Stop saying those things and listen to me. No one ever touched me."

"Don't you raise your voice to your father," Marilyn Carver said coldly.

"Let me tell you what happened," Misty pleaded, her voice rising in desperation.

"I don't want you talking in front of your mother about what you did with that boy!" her father roared.

"Listen to me. I didn't do anything." Misty's voice quavered.

"Slut, slut," her father bellowed.

"I'm not, I'm not . . ."

In her dream, her father's face grew and grew and became distorted into a grotesque mask. Then she saw herself standing between Aunt Lizabeth and Uncle Charles, her parents facing them, her gaze going from one couple to the other.

"I don't care if you are my brother," said Aunt Lizabeth, "I won't let you do this to her anymore."

"I tell you she had an abortion," her father yelled.

"How do you know that? Has she ever been examined by a doctor?" her aunt shot back.

"No," Misty answered softly. "Never."

"Misty, be quiet," her mother said through pursed lips. "Don't interrupt. Nice girls do not speak until they are spoken to."

"You never talk to me," Misty told her mother, earning a glare from her father.

Aunt Lizabeth and her father argued for hours. In the end it was decided that Misty would stay in school but live with her aunt and uncle.

In the car on the way to Misty's new home, her aunt had looked over the seat at Misty huddled in the back. "No wonder you called me, child. Now, don't you worry. We have a piano, so you can practice at home instead of going to the music room at school after classes. Why did that fool brother of mine sell the piano?"

"Mama told him it disturbed her, and he said he didn't like the noise, either."

"Damn fools, both of them," her uncle muttered.

"Charlie, there's no need to swear," Aunt Lizabeth said mildly as Misty was jostled in the back seat by the car's movements.

Gradually she emerged from the depth of sleep and realized someone was gently shaking her shoulder. "Come on, darling, wake up. We're here." Luc frowned down at her and gently pushed curling tendrils of red-gold hair away from her forehead.

What was wrong? Misty tried to clear her sleep-befuddled mind. Why was Luc scowling at her like that? She became instinctively defensive. "We can always turn around and drive back," she told him sharply. "I'll pick up the girls at your sister's house—"

"What are you babbling about, love?" he interrupted, helping her out of the car and taking her arm to lead her through the gate in a picket fence.

But now Misty was wide awake. She paused to admire the series of humpbacked mountains that circled the town of Hudson. "They're beautiful," she murmured.

Luc pointed toward the distance. "Do you see that bare snakelike area on that mountainside? That's Sweetgum, the ski resort where we'll be staying tonight."

Suddenly Misty knew she couldn't go through with the marriage. Panic churned inside her. She inhaled deeply of the crisp winter air and turned resolutely to face him. "Listen to me, Luc. This marriage is a mistake. We can't do it."

The words seemed to echo in the cold air. "I . . . I've been through two failed relationships." Her eyes slid away from his.

"I know all about that." He led her up several steps to a wraparound porch with a grass doormat in front of the oak door. A sign pasted to the glass window said Enter.

Misty stopped in her tracks. "Come on, darling," Luc said in low tones.

"I've never done anything like this before," she muttered, dragging her heels.

"Neither have I," he said, opening the door and waiting for her to precede him inside.

"That's true." For some reason his words sent an unaccountable feeling of relief through her. "We can help each other during the hard parts," she said.

"That's my thought exactly."

A plump woman well past middle age came forward from a back room to greet them. She was wearing a gray dress with a white lace collar and cuffs. "Hello, I'm Judge Latimer. You must be Lucas Harrison and Mystique Carver."

"Yes," Luc answered for both of them, removing the jacket from Misty's shoulders.

She was about to explain that Mystique wasn't her real name, then decided that if that's what Luc liked to call her, she might as well let him.

Judge Latimer led them into a spacious parlor with a bay window in which a marmalade cat sat washing its paws. It looked up briefly at the company, then resumed it's methodical licking. "I've arranged for my housekeeper and my lawyer to serve as witnesses to the ceremony. Is that all right with you?" asked the judge.

"Of course," Luc said, his hot gaze roving over Misty. "You look lovely, darling." He slid an arm around her waist and hugged her to him as the judge excused herself. "Here. I have something for you." He took a jeweler's box from his pocket and handed it to her.

Misty stared at it in confusion. "I can't put the wedding band on until the judge—"

"This is your engagement ring," he told her, leaning forward to let his mouth graze hers.

"We're not engaged. I mean, I don't need one."

"Indulge me by wearing it," Luc whispered into her hair as he lifted her right hand and slipped a square-cut emerald on her finger. "Do you like it?"

Misty slowly lifted her hand, letting the stone catch a ray of late afternoon sunlight. "It looks too large to be real."

Luc laughed. "It's real, all right."

"Don't do too much for me," Misty requested, overwhelmed by everything that had happened that day. How could she explain to Luc that she feared becoming too dependent on him? Not because of the material things he could give her, but because the sweetness and passion he had shown her were already binding her to him irrevocably. If, later on, he took away the caring, withdrew the tenderness, she would be utterly bereft.

"I am giving you my life this afternoon. What you do with it is up to you," he said solemnly, his eyes holding hers, his hand clasped warmly in her own.

"It will be spoiled," Misty said with a moan, shutting her eyes in momentary pain, her left hand coming over to protectively cover her right one.

She felt Luc's hand grasp her shoulders to draw her close just as Judge Latimer returned with a balding man and a thin woman, both middle-aged.

"Mr. Harrison, Miss Carver, this is George Lemond, my lawyer, and this is Esther Gregson, my housekeeper. Shall we begin?" Judge Latimer pressed a button on a stereo system, and Mendelssohn's Wedding March played softly in the background.

Following the judge's instructions, Misty and Luc took their places side by side in front of the fireplace between the two witnesses. Judge Latimer faced them.

"Dearly beloved," the judge began, "we are gathered here . . ."

Misty supposed the judge must be speaking because her mouth was moving, but Misty couldn't hear over the roaring in her ears. Her eyes didn't seem to be focusing properly. Blinking to keep the judge's face from becoming blurry, she was grateful for the strong grip of Luc's hand in hers.

When he looked down with one eyebrow arched, Misty knew he wanted her to respond to the judge's query. "I do," Misty said. He smiled with what looked like relief and squeezed her hand. Misty watched his mouth move in response, reading his lips as he repeated his vows. The roaring in her ears faded away.

"Now, by the power vested in me by the sovereign state of New York, I pronounce you husband and wife." Judge Latimer beamed at them as Luc bent to kiss her.

"I will make you happy, darling," he promised against her lips.

"Thank you," Misty said, and then she felt silly at her inappropriate remark. Her smile slipped on and off her face.

Congratulations were spoken all around, and Mrs. Gregson produced a bottle of New York State blanc de blanc with which to toast the bride and groom.

Soon they were saying good-bye and Luc was leading Misty out onto the porch. He insisted that she button her jacket up to the neck.

"I don't care if the fur tickles you; you have to keep warm," he insisted. "It's colder up here, but you don't notice it because the air is so dry." He frowned down at her feet. "I should have insisted that you wear boots instead of those pumps."

"Don't be silly. The car is warm," she answered as Luc hurried her into the front seat and started the engine. All at once she remembered something. "I put a ring on your finger. I didn't know you were going to wear a wedding ring."

Luc held out his hand to show her the heavy gold band, which exactly matched her own. "I decided I'd like to wear one. Do you mind?"

"Oh, no. I'm glad. I mean, it's a very nice ring."

"Yes, it is. So is yours. Are you going to put your engagement ring on your left hand now?"

"Ah . . ." Misty held out both hands. "No, I think I'll wear them this way. Then my wedding ring won't be overshadowed by the emerald."

Luc threw back his head and laughed as the car shot forward. "You also have emerald earrings coming to you, my pet." He glanced at her. "I called you on Christmas Day to see if you liked them, but you weren't home."

"I was at Aileen and Dave's."

"Then you sent the earrings back to me." He shook his

head. "That angered and confused me." Suddenly he smiled. "But now you're getting them back."

Misty glanced at him. "Why don't you keep them?" she suggested, laughing out loud for no particular reason. She was still chuckling when she noticed that Luc was giving her peculiar glances. "What is it?" she asked. "Did I say something?"

"No, my lovely wife, it's your laugh. I haven't heard it enough. I find that I want to hear it as often as possible."

Misty sighed. "I really like to laugh."

"But that wistful note in your voice tells me you don't do it often enough."

Misty didn't answer him. Her attention was taken by the narrow, winding road that was leading them into the mountains. "Look at all the snow!" she exclaimed. Snow had often fallen in the area where she was raised, but it had never looked so white and sparkling.

As they rounded a curve at the top of a driveway, the Sweetgum Inn appeared like a jewel in the snow.

"Luc, it's perfect," Misty whispered, staring at the rough-hewn exterior that had weathered to a deep brown. The rambling building had an open front porch, and smoke was coming from a stone chimney.

"We'll eat here, but we'll stay in one of the guest cottages," Luc told her, grinning at her wide-eyed expression. He parked the car in front of the entrance.

Luc came around to her side of the car and reached in to help her to her feet. "Like it?" he asked.

She nodded, then pointed. "Oh, look! Skiers." She shaded her eyes against the rays of the dying sun and watched black dots sliding down the slopes. "I think I would like to try," she said.

"Then we will."

"But I haven't got any ski clothes," she pointed out as he led her up the steps to the front door, gesturing to a bellman to carry their luggage. She gasped at the amount of baggage being pulled out of the car. "We have a great deal for just one night."

"Yes." He grinned unrepentantly at her.

"You bought me clothes," she accused as he shepherded her through the lobby. "Oooh, it's nice." Immediately forgetting her quarrel with him, she gazed around her, her attention caught by the knotty-pine interior of the lodge. Tables and chairs were grouped casually throughout the spacious lobby.

"Mr. Harrison, welcome back to the Sweetgum Inn," said the smiling desk clerk, nodding to Luc and running curious eyes over Misty.

"My wife and I will be staying a day or two," Luc said, signing the register.

"Your wife?" The clerk looked momentarily discomfited. "May we at the Sweetgum Inn wish you well, sir?"

"Thank you. We were married today." Luc's mouth lifted at the corners as he glanced at a blushing Misty. "I'd like some ski attire sent to our cabin for my wife. Size six in clothing, size seven in boots."

"Of course, sir." The man bowed slightly and signaled to a bellman.

Misty stopped often on her way to the guest cottage to gaze, fascinated, at the skiers coming down the mountain and at the powdery snow that covered the trees and crunched under their feet.

Luc put his arm around her and hurried her along. "Come on. Your feet will get cold."

The bellman opened the door of their cottage, which was actually a small bungalow. It had a bedroom, living room, kitchen, and dining area, plus a picture window that looked out over the mountains.

"Oh, a fire in the fireplace." Misty sighed as Luc removed her fur coat, then sat her down to remove her shoes and rub her feet. He tipped the bellman and came back to her as she sat on the low couch in front of the roaring blaze.

"It's beautiful, Luc."

"I've never stayed in this cottage before, because I thought it was too big for just me."

"You and your stable of women," Misty heard herself say tartly in a voice she didn't recognize as her own.

Luc turned toward her, his eyes searing into her. "There's no need to be jealous about my past, darling. I'm not jealous of yours."

"Neither am I," she shot back, coming to a ramrod straight position on the overstuffed couch. "I . . . I have never discussed Leonard or Richard with you."

"Now is not the time," Luc said, throwing his suit jacket toward a chair, not noticing when it fell to the floor. He loosened his tie and jerked it off. "We'll have plenty of time to talk, darling. The rest of our lives, in fact. But right now I want to love you, to show you how I feel. I want you to know how much I need you."

Misty's heart began pounding as he unbuttoned his shirt and pulled it off his powerful shoulders.

CHAPTER FIVE

IN THE NEXT instant Luc lifted her into his arms and carried her to the spacious bedroom decorated in peach and brown tones. Sudden shyness overcame her as he placed her on the peach-colored bedspread covering the king-sized bed. She felt her face redden. Something about making love with Luc embarrassed her. Sex with Richard and Leonard had been a mechanical act that didn't involve her mind and spirit. But she knew instinctively that Luc would demand all of her, heart and soul. The idea of such total intimacy with him made her flush with both reluctance and anticipation as he followed her down onto the bed, pressing her into the firm mattress.

He quizzically regarded the heightened color in her face. "Mrs. Harrison, do you mind that I'm going to undress you?"

"No," she whispered. *But I do mind*, an inner voice shouted. With Richard and Leonard she'd always undressed in the bathroom, and she'd worn a robe until she climbed into bed. With them, sex had been an obligation, and not a completely comfortable one . . .

"Good, because I'm going to enjoy this, my sweet," Luc

murmured. "And so are you." His voice was thick as he peeled the pantyhose down her legs. "You know, my love, I think I'm going to buy you some underthings with garters. I saw some in Saks that would be perfect for you." He lifted her hips and slid the skirt down her body. "Ummm, pretty panties." He kissed the silken briefs, pressing his open mouth to her pelvic area in a caress that awakened a slow throbbing.

Misty gasped, and her body moved involuntarily in surprise at his tender loving. No one had ever kissed her like that! She was stunned. A tingling sensation began in her hands and feet as Luc raised her to a sitting position and removed her cream-colored jacket and the frilly blouse with the lace jabot.

"Pretty bra, darling." He ran a gentle finger around the embroidered edge. "Did I buy you this one?"

"Yes," she said breathlessly as he reached down and unfastened the tiny clip between her breasts. His mouth followed his hand, his arm supporting her arching back. Her hands came up to grasp his hair, her fingers threading through the thick locks.

"You're so sweet, wife of mine." Luc lifted her up against his body with ease, suspending her with one arm, taking her breast more fully into his mouth and with infinite tenderness sucking slowly, sweetly.

"Luc!" Misty cried out, her hands clenching in his hair, her eyes closing as hot, pulsing sensations seared through her. "What . . . what . . ." She tried to speak, but her mouth couldn't form the words.

"Shhh, my angel. Let me love you." Luc's hoarse words sent a thousand tiny electrical charges over her skin, like lightning bouncing off mountaintops. He pressed her down, down onto the peach coverlet. "Let me cover you . . ."

"I'm warm," Misty said with a gasp. "I don't need any covers." Her hands slid free of him, her fingers clutching air as he stepped away to remove his trousers and briefs. Her body tingled with delight as she stared up at him—at the thicket of chestnut hair that arrowed down his body, the color a surprising contrast to the ash blond locks on his head. Her sisters would describe him as a hunk, Misty thought giddily. His legs were long and muscular, his shoulders broad and powerful. At this moment he looked every inch the athlete Aileen had said he was. Misty reached for him again.

"Easy, darling, I'm not leaving you," he crooned, stretching out at her side.

"I love your hair," she whispered, reaching again for his head, her fingers spreading and closing in delight at touching him.

"Good. I love everything about you," he murmured back, sliding his mouth down her body, touching every inch, caressing every curve, exploring every intimate crevice. His mouth traveled lower and lower, and then he was touching the very core of her desire, setting off a kaleidoscope of overwhelming feelings. Her blood seemed to turn to molten lava in her veins. She trembled and writhed in uncontrollable passion.

"Shhh, darling. I'm loving you."

"Ohhh..." She pulled his hair, impatient with him, but he merely chuckled against her skin. She pulled harder, and he inched upward until they were touching lips to lips. "I didn't realize," she whispered, awed.

"I know, my treasure." He pressed her thighs farther apart and positioned himself over her. "I'm glad, because I want to be your first real lover." He pushed himself gently into her.

His heart was pounding against hers. Her breath was coming in staccato gasps as the tempo between them increased. Never had Misty been an eager participant, but now she clasped her lover and held him tight. Together they soared, higher and higher, until the world exploded, flinging them up to the stars, around the sun, and gently back down to earth.

For long moments afterward they held each other tightly. Gradually their breathing slowed, their glistening bodies relaxed.

"Does anyone know about this but us?" Misty whispered up at Luc, her eyelids drooping.

"About what, Mystique?" He nibbled at her neck.

"About... about lovemaking?"

Luc chuckled and raised himself on one elbow to look

down at her. "I doubt it," he teased. "Shall we make it our secret?"

"Yes!" But her laughter vanished as his grin faded. "What is it? Why are you looking at me like that?"

"I told you before, I love to hear you laugh."

"I feel like laughing. In fact, I wish we had a piano so I could play and we could sing." Feeling sleepy, she burrowed her nose into his neck.

"Going to sleep on me?"

"Yes," she admitted with a tiny smile.

"I forgot to tell you that that was only the beginning. I intend to make love to you all night." He took her earlobe between his teeth.

"Wonderful. Don't start without me," she muttered, yawning.

"Don't worry, I won't." He chuckled again. "I've never laughed quite so much either, my little wife," he whispered, pulling her closer to him and closing his eyes.

In the night Misty dreamed again. She saw her father coming toward her, ever closer. But when she called out, Luc was there, and her father vanished in an instant. She sank deeper into sleep.

Later, Misty smiled, her eyes closed, as she felt soft kisses on her neck and face. "Luc," she murmured.

"Yes, my darling wife, it's Luc," he murmured gently.

She felt his mouth move lower, caressing her breasts and arms. Her body wriggled in response, but still she didn't open her eyes. She had the irrational feeling that, if she looked, Luc wouldn't really be there, and that she would find that she had only imagined the ecstasy of their wedding night. Beautiful, wondrous emotions had cascaded over her. It would be terrible to wake up and find he had been just a figment of her imagination. But once again he proved his existence with the reality of his lovemaking.

His hands coursed down one side of her body and began working their way up the other. He gently bit each toe. His mouth massaged each kneecap. He nuzzled her thighs with his mouth in a tender quest. He kissed her arms, her fingertips, and the crook of each elbow with special loving attention. He was nibbling her chin when she opened one eye.

"Don't be a ghost, Luc," she whispered.

"I'm not," he assured her. "Open both your eyes, Mystique."

"All right." She opened them and sighed. He wasn't a ghost; he was real. With a deep, shuddering breath she touched his cheek with her fingertips.

"Do you mind if I continue to enjoy my breakfast?" he teased with a wicked gleam in his eyes.

"Am I sunny-side up?" She smiled at him. Then she felt herself being lifted and turned over, face down in the pillow.

"Now you're sunny-side up, angel. Ummm, how luscious." Luc nipped at her backside, his open mouth gentle on her scars. He explored her back from her neck to her ankles, setting her on fire.

When he turned her over once again to enter her body, Misty was ready for him, eager to be swallowed by the hot, piercing rhythm they created together.

They strove mightily to give the other the utmost satisfaction, and once again the world exploded. They lay close together, open mouth on open mouth, their eyelids fluttering, their breath mingling.

"My goodness." Misty gazed lovingly at her husband. "That was more powerful than anything on earth."

"Yes." His brown eyes were somber for a moment; then he smiled and rolled from the bed to pull her to her feet. "Let's take a shower."

"Together?" Misty asked, recalling how Leonard had always insisted on having the bathroom first, leaving her to clean up after him.

"Forget them," Luc growled, reading her thoughts and pulling her to him in a fierce embrace. "You're thinking of those two fools. Don't. I don't want to be compared to them."

"That would be impossible. You'd get a nosebleed if you dropped down to their level," Misty said, the words popping out before she could stop them. She felt her face flush.

Luc chuckled and kissed her cheek. "Mystique, that was a sweet thing to say. I think I'll run out in the snow and thump my chest."

"Not without clothes on, you won't." She took a deep breath. "I won't let you."

"Lord, I've married a bossy wife!" Luc lifted her in his arms and carried her into the bathroom.

"Yes," she said firmly, marveling at her own daring as she clung to his neck, not letting go even when he let her slide down his body. He turned the spigots in the shower stall. "Will we fit?" she asked, laughing again. She had never laughed or giggled so much! Luc would begin to think she was silly.

"Of course we'll fit." He watched with lazy amusement and flinched from the cold spray. After readjusting the knobs, he tested the water. "There." He lifted her into the stall and stepped in himself. "Isn't this nice?"

"Yes," she said softly, loving the feel of his hard-muscled body against hers. "Luc . . ." She lifted her head to look at him as he began running a loofah sponge down her arm.

"Uh-huh?" He seemed to be completely absorbed in the task.

"Don't stay with me when we go skiing today. I'll get an instructor to teach me."

He handed her the loofah, and stood still while she scrubbed him. "I've already arranged for an instructor, Debbie Allen, to give you a preliminary lesson. Then I'll take over." His eyes went to her breasts as she raised her arms to rinse the soap from her body. "Darling, are you finished? Good, because I think you'd better get out of here if you want to go skiing today." His eyes glinted with laughter as her eyes darted away from the most blatant sign of his obvious arousal. "I'm beginning to think I may have to move my office to our house."

"Would you like to postpone skiing?" she asked, stepping out of the shower stall and taking a towel from the warming rack. Skillfully she wrapped it around her body like a sarong.

"Yes, I would." He closed the shower door with a snap, then abruptly opened it again. "Don't think I don't know you're teasing me, wife." He grinned at her and banged the door shut once more.

Misty skipped into the bedroom, hugging herself. This can't be happening to me, she thought. Luc can't be real.

She was standing in her bra and panties in the bedroom

when he came out of the bathroom, naked and rubbing his hair with a towel. She smiled, then laughed out loud when he closed his eyes and groaned. In a few swift strides he closed the space between them, a determined expression on his face.

"Skiing," Misty muttered, laughing.

"Skiing, hell," Luc snarled, scooping her up into his arms. "How can you stand there in those peach-colored underthings and expect me to go skiing? It's insanity." He carried her to the bed.

"Luc, you haven't had breakfast yet," she protested laughing.

"Tell me about it," he muttered into her skin, removing the bits of lace from her body.

The fire storm took them again, yet to Misty it seemed brand-new—fresh and exhilarating. Afterward, she was sure she must have misunderstood the words Luc murmured against her flushed skin. He couldn't have said he loved her, could he?

They were holding each other, their hands sliding over each other's bodies, waiting for the love tremors to subside, when a knock sounded at the door. "Mrs. Harrison, I have your ski clothing," said a voice muffled by the door.

With a sharp yelp, Misty jumped out of bed and streaked into the bathroom. When Luc handed her a pair of slacks and a shirt through a crack in the door, she poked her tongue out at him.

"Don't do that, love," he warned, "or we'll be back in bed again before you know it." She gasped, and he chuckled.

"Answer that door," she told him.

It didn't take long to try on the skiing togs, but Misty was surprised at how picky Luc was about everything for her. At last, after the bellman left, they finished getting dressed, Luc's eyes going over her in lazy assessment of everything that came into his view. "You are one beautiful woman, Mystique Harrison. Even in those skiing togs you send me into a spin."

Misty looked down at her pale green ski outfit, which felt incredibly warm but as light as a feather. She moved her feet in the heavy green ski boots.

Luc, dressed all in black with black goggles dangling

from one hand, ran his other hand over her short battle jacket. "The man at the desk assured me that this was the lightest, warmest outfit. How do your long johns feel?"

"Comfy." Misty wriggled inside her suit.

"You look damn sexy, too, my little siren," Luc said in low tones. "Here, these are your goggles, and I want you to wear them. The lenses are tinted to prevent glare, but they also react to growing darkness and allow clearer night vision."

"The wonders of science," Misty murmured, hooking her gloves onto her sleeves in the way Luc had shown her and placing her hand in his as they left the cottage and walked the short distance to the lodge.

Misty inhaled deeply of the numbing air, feeling warm and comfortable in her thermal clothes. "My goodness." She pointed to the chair lift rising up the mountainside. "That looks as though it's going up at an awfully steep angle."

"It is," Luc agreed, watching her. "The ride up can be cold, but coming down makes it all worthwhile. Here, let me take you over to the instructor's office and get you settled."

"No," Misty said, "it's right there." She pointed to a small shed attached to the back of the lodge. "You go ahead and get some skiing in while the sun is still shining. I'll be fine."

"You're sure?" Luc kissed her and glanced around him as if searching for hidden dangers. He scowled at several skiers who were lounging near an outdoor stove, then looked back at Misty.

"I'll be fine," she repeated, giving him a slight shove. After kissing her again, he reluctantly left her.

She went to the open window of the instructors' office. Seeing no one, she called, "Hello, I'm Misty Car—Harrison. I'm supposed to have a lesson with Debbie Allen."

A tall blond man came up to the window. "I'm Roger Larsen, Mrs. Harrison. Debbie isn't finished teaching her youth group yet, so I'll be your instructor this morning." He smiled broadly, deepening the dimples at the side of his mouth and making his widely spaced blue eyes twinkle.

Misty decided she preferred tall, athletic men with ash blond hair and brown eyes.

"Ah, fine," she said. "Shall we go out now?"

"Just let me get my gear."

Roger demonstrated several basic maneuvers—the snowplow, a simple stem christie, and paralleling—on a slight incline nearby. As Misty gained confidence, they progressed to a more advanced beginners' slope. Roger skied closer to her as she tried to put her lessons into practice.

Misty grew exhilarated as she continued to ski without falling and was able to perform most of the turns with ease. Soon she was eager to try the rope tow that would take them up an even longer and slightly more precipitous incline.

She fell on the rope tow, receiving a faceful of snow, but she held on steadfastly until they reached the crest of the hill. "I really don't like that rope tow," she told Roger. "I suppose I will *hate* the chair lift."

Roger laughed. "Don't worry. You'll like the chairs better. But we'll try this hill a few times first."

Misty was amazed and pleased at how rapidly she progressed under Roger's instruction. As she skied down the gentle slope, she was delighted with the sensation of flying through space.

"Now we'll try the chairs." But Roger fell abruptly silent as he gazed past her shoulder, a wrinkle of puzzlement in his forehead. Misty turned to see Luc striding toward them, looking like the very devil in his black attire. His mouth was a tight slash in his face, and his hair shone silver in the sunlight.

"Mystique," he said angrily, tearing the goggles from his face and glaring at Roger. "Where is your ski instructor?"

"Debbie was still with her youth group, so I volunteered to instruct your daughter, sir," Roger explained.

Luc seemed to swell with anger.

"Luc, you look like Darth Vader," Misty exclaimed, then clamped a mittened hand over her mouth when Luc's head swung abruptly toward her. "Ah, thank you for the lessons, Roger," she called. "We have to go." She pushed her poles into the snow and glided forward—straight into Luc! He caught her with his hands, struggling to maintain their balance. "Thank you." Misty leaned up and kissed Luc's chin, confirming with a quick sideways glance that Roger was skiing away from them.

"Where the hell does he get off—" Luc fumed, glaring after Roger, his arms around Misty.

"He was only teaching me to snowplow and stem christie, and tomorrow he wanted to show me—"

"I'll be teaching you tomorrow," Luc said firmly, his hands tightening on her. He brought icy lips down on hers. "Damn him," he said against her mouth before lifting his lips a fraction of an inch. "Thinking I was your father. I'll kill him." He ran his ungloved hand down her cheek. "You do look young. No more than seventeen."

Misty leaned against him, reveling in his warmth as his body sheltered her from the wind. "Roger's harmless," she assured her husband.

"Ha!" Luc laughed harshly and leaned over Misty, his body shielding her. "Are you warm enough? Would you like to go inside the lodge and get some soup?"

She did feel a little damp, but she was eager to show Luc what she'd learned so far. "I'd like to go up on the chair lift and ski down that slope first."

Luc studied her for a moment and finally nodded. He checked to see that her poles were in the proper position and skied with her to the end of the short line of skiers waiting for the lift. A stiff breeze momentarily chilled her. "Did you just shiver?" he demanded.

"Uh-uh," Misty lied, sensing that Luc would whisk her back to the lodge in a moment if she gave him the slightest indication that she was cold.

But she hadn't anticipated the blasts of frigid air that assailed her on the chair lift. Although she and Luc went to only one of the intermediate hills, the frosty wind left her stiff and chilled when she alighted with Luc's help.

"You *are* cold," he accused her. "Your lips are turning blue. Damn you, Mystique."

"I'll be better once we get moving," she said, trying to control the shivers that wracked her body. Turning away from Luc, she skied toward the lip of the hill. Looking down, she felt sure that the descent would be relatively easy, even for a beginner like herself. But the cold had begun to stiffen her hands, and her feet were chilled. She pushed off, wanting to get down to the bottom and into the warm lodge as soon as possible.

"Mystique!" Luc called from behind her, alarm in his voice.

Abruptly Misty forgot how cold she was in the stunning realization that she was going to need all her concentration to get down the slope without falling. She was moving faster than she cared to. "Plow, darling, plow," Luc called. "That's it . . . good. Now traverse. That's fine."

Suddenly he was at her side, guiding her past a group of skiers. Sudden confidence infused Misty. Luc was there! He wouldn't let anything happen to her.

Cautiously she tried to parallel. But her left ski slipped, and she felt herself falling. The heel and toe bindings on her left ski came undone, and she tumbled several yards down the hill, the collar of her jacket filling with snow, her face pushing through the soft powder. She was laughing as she raised herself from a snow bank.

Before she could stand up, Luc was taking her in his arms and lifting her high. "Darling, are you all right? I shouldn't have let you do it." Cradling her close with one arm, he wiped her face with his other hand.

"Ptui." Misty giggled. "Will Sweetgum Inn charge you extra because I'm eating up all their powder?"

The beginning of a smile softened Luc's rocklike visage. "You're a good sport." He kissed her nose, then placed her on her feet. "Come on. Let's get down this hill."

Misty helped Luc brush the snow from her clothes. "I want to ski down, Luc. Please. It isn't far."

"All right. But traverse." She nodded, brushing some snow off him.

Luc stuck to her like glue the rest of the way down the hill, talking to her, encouraging her, instructing her in soft, sure tones.

When Misty reached the bottom, she wobbled, then regained her balance and came to a full stop facing Luc. "I did it!" she exclaimed, grinning and shivering at the same time.

Luc scowled at her, gestured to an attendant, kicked off his skis, and loosened hers. In seconds he was hurrying her into the lodge. "But Luc, you can't walk away and leave our stuff out there," Misty protested. She looked over her shoulder to see if the young attendant was giving proper attention to Luc's equipment.

"Never mind that. I have to get you inside."

Another attendant rushed forward as Luc half lifted her, hustling her through the doorway into the basement ski room. A group of skiers was clustered around a blazing fire in a rough-hewn stone fireplace. "Was there an accident?" a young man asked anxiously.

"No, of course not," Misty denied, whispering furiously at Luc to let her go.

"My wife is cold," he said. "I want some soup and hot chocolate *now*." He turned to glare at the people sitting on a couch next to the fire.

"Stop that," Misty exclaimed. "You can't act like Attila the Hun in here." A flush of embarrassment warmed her cheeks as three people scrambled up from the sofa.

"Put her here," one offered.

"She can have my spot," said another.

"Did she fall?" asked the third. "Has she seen a doctor?"

"Luc," Misty said with a moan as he settled her on the couch and unfastened her boots. She looked up at a semi-circle of concerned expressions and tried to smile. "I'm fine," she said weakly.

"She's very cold," Luc said, as if accusing the world. He rubbed her bare foot, then blew on it.

"Stop," Misty said with a gasp, feeling tendrils of warmth begin to uncurl deep inside her. "You're tickling me."

"Am I, darling?" He caressed her with his eyes.

Misty tried to sink deeper into the cushions. "Have you no shame?" she whispered with a forced, lopsided smile.

A young red-haired man hurried up to them, carrying a bucket of warm water. "Here. This will help," he said, lifting one of Misty's hands and plunging it into the water. "We have to gradually heat the extremities, you know." He stared at Misty wide-eyed. "I put baby oil in the water so your hands won't be chapped."

Misty smiled weakly. "That was very kind of you."

Someone bustled up carrying a small tureen of soup.

Another hurried over with hot chocolate in a white china mug.

"Luc," Misty begged. "Stop this."

He looked up at her with surprise, then glanced around the room. "Stop what, love?"

Lord, she had married a sweet despot! Luc was so used to having people jump up and run errands for him, that he saw nothing out of the ordinary in being waited on. When he took the soup spoon and tried to feed her, she glared furiously at him. "That's enough," she snapped, snatching the spoon from his hand.

"Poor thing is still jumpy," someone said sympathetically.

"Yes, it must be nerves," another concurred.

"I'm fine," Misty insisted, her exasperation turning to resignation. She looked into the depths of the vegetable soup and raised a spoonful to her lips. It was good. She tasted several more spoonfuls, then took a tentative sip from the mug of hot chocolate, assuring everyone between sips that she really didn't want anything else.

Almost half an hour went by before people began to disperse. "Luc," Misty said, feeling exhausted from all the attention, "I'd like to go back to our cottage now."

"Are you sure you're strong enough?" He ran a worried glance over her.

"If I were any stronger, I'd be pulling a trolley car in San Francisco," she retorted.

Luc's eyes narrowed on her momentarily. Then a smile lifted the corners of his mouth. "Irked with me, love?"

"Yes," she declared, swinging her legs off the couch and getting to her feet, resisting with effort the urge to jerk her arm free of his hold.

"Sorry, but you'll have to get used to it. I'm not letting anything happen to you."

"Must I remind you that I'm not helpless? I've been on my own for some time now and—"

"You're my darling." Luc fastened her jacket and kissed the tip of her nose. Then he dropped down to the floor and lifted each foot to put on her boots.

Misty balanced herself by placing one hand on his head.

She was torn between the longing to savor the tactile delight of Luc's crisp, clean hair and the irritated urge to give his head a good yank.

They said good-bye to all the people who had been so concerned about Misty. Luc seemed to feel none of the embarrassment she experienced. He promised that he and his wife would meet them for a drink if they decided to stay an extra night.

On the short walk back to their cottage, Luc kept his arm tightly around her, now and then pressing his lips to her hair. Misty felt as though she were traveling in a pink bubble that they alone inhabited. "Luc, you mustn't worry about me," she said, forgetting her irritation in the relaxing aura of his presence.

"I can't seem to help it, my dear." He gave her a bittersweet smile. "Marriage is proving to be tougher and more complicated that I ever imagined."

Misty stared up at him as he held the door open for her. A shiver of panic zigzagged down her spine. Was he already regretting their marriage? Never! She wouldn't let him! He was hers now. She stood in the center of the living room, staring at the empty fireplace, crossing her arms in front of her, hugging the pain to her. Blinking, she watched Luc bend to light a fire. Soon a roaring blaze was radiating heat into the room. But still Misty didn't move.

"Hey, what's so interesting in those flames that you can't tear your eyes away?" Luc asked, lifting her chin and staring down into her eyes. "I'll be back in a moment. I'm going to run a bath for you."

Still Misty didn't move. I really can't survive without him now, she thought. Damn him. I hate him for making me love him. Why did he have to make himself such an important part of my life? There won't be anything left of me if he ever goes away. Damn him!

Luc came back into the room. He paused momentarily on the threshold, studying her. "I should never have let you get so chilled," he said grimly. "Come on, darling." Misty went with him, loving the feel of his warm body as he led her into the bathroom, keeping her close to his side. "Have I told you yet that I enjoy undressing you?" he asked, removing her clothes in the steamy warmth of the good-sized room.

"I like sunken bathtubs," she mused, feeling a sense of defeat because she couldn't muster the strength to tell Luc to get lost . . . before he took over her life completely. She'd been able to do it with Leonard and Richard. Even with her father she'd summoned up the courage to ask to live with her aunt and uncle. Now she had a feeling of falling through space, of spiraling down toward the crash that would inevitably come when Luc left her. Until then, she was helpless to erect barriers between them to protect her emotions against him.

She looked down at him as he rolled her long johns down her legs. Damn you to hell, Lucas Stuyvesant Harrison. You've hooked me like a fish and thrown me into the boat. I'm yours until you toss me back into the water. How did you manage to soften my backbone? I used to be so full of fight.

"Darling? Darling, are you daydreaming? Not that I don't want you to, but I'd rather you concentrated on me." Luc leaned forward from his kneeling position and kissed her navel. "Because I sure as hell can't think of anyone but you."

"That will pass," Misty mumbled as she slid into the tub.

"What did you say?" Abruptly he stood to remove his clothes and stepped into the tub with her. "Whew, isn't this too hot for you?"

"No, it's nice." She closed her eyes and leaned against his chest, opened one eye and noticed an array of powders and oils on the shelf next to the tub. "What's this?" She raised a languid arm and grasped a tall plastic bottle. "My goodness. Opium is a perfume. I didn't know they made a bath oil, too. You'll like this, Luc."

"Mystique, for God's sake don't—" Luc half laughed, half groaned as she poured the fragrant liquid into the tub.

"Aren't we sweet?" she simpered.

"You little devil. I should paddle your bottom."

"Lovely." She looked up at him, wide-eyed. "Why not?"

Luc stared down at her for long moments, his skin flushed.

"And when did you turn into Circe?" he quizzed hoarsely.

"The minute you married me, I think," Misty muttered, watching his face come closer.

"I agree." His mouth teased her lips apart. "I want to have you all the time." She caught a note of disbelief in his voice, as though such a realization had shaken him.

"I want you all the time, too, Luc," she admitted.

"Darling . . ." He pulled her on top of him and massaged her backside with gentle, possessive strokes, his teeth nibbling at her neck. "You're so sweet. Each day I learn something new about you."

"Me, too."

"You find something new about you every day?" Luc chuckled and buried his face in her hair.

"Not about me, about you." Her fingers kneaded the muscled flesh of his shoulders. Erotic sensations flooded through her as she explored his chest and lower body.

"Yes," Luc said, his face still in her hair. "Touch me, love. I want you to."

Misty had never especially wanted to touch either Richard or Leonard. With them, she had tried to convince herself that sex wasn't particularly important. Having similar goals, tastes, and ideas about life were of paramount importance.

But now! Every pore of Luc's body hypnotized her. "You're gorgeous," she whispered. "I don't think men are supposed to be so gorgeous."

"I never want you to stop thinking that . . . Ohhh, Mystique, don't stop. That feels so good."

Luc's own hands became busy on her body. Misty felt a familiar heat begin to spread deep inside her. Her flesh became a liquid flame. Her pulse sped out of control. Her breath grew harsh and heavy. "Luc, you're teasing me." She clasped him fiercely, exulting when she heard him groan.

He rose abruptly to his feet, wrapped them both in huge towels, and hurried her to the bedroom. Their love play became fire play as both of them went up in flames of passion.

"Darling . . . not so fast. I can't . . ." Luc's face was a mask of sensual feeling, his cheeks crimson with blood, his eyes glazed with passion.

"Luc!" Misty heard the hoarseness in her voice when she

called out to him. She was awed by the power of feeling between them.

Once again they scaled the heights to a peak of emotion and fell back exhausted, still clutching each other fiercely.

"I never wanted anything so much in my life as to satisfy you in our lovemaking," Luc murmured against her breasts. "I've wanted that since the first moment I saw you."

"You have satisfied me," Misty whispered, her eyes heavy with contented weariness.

"Your eyes are like dewy green violets," Luc said. His grin was lopsided, as though he were trying to hide the tumult only now subsiding inside him.

"I thought you were a banker, not a poet." Misty ran her fingernail lightly down his nose.

"I'm finding that, since meeting you, wife, I've become a multifaceted person." He took a deep breath. "I find that I want to tell you things I've never considered telling anyone else. You've changed me. I'd heard of sensual love, but I didn't believe it really existed. I never believed that anyone could take over my life, yet at the same time fulfill it with beauty and warmth." His body shuddered as he drew in an unsteady breath. "There were always women. They were as matter-of-fact about sex as I was. I was certain that was all there was to it . . . until the night I first saw you playing the piano. You turned my life upside down."

Misty giggled and snuggled closer to him.

He took all her weight on top of him and pulled the satin quilt over her back. "Shall we stay one more day?"

"I can't. I have to work tomorrow night."

"Have you forgotten that you're now part owner of the Terrace Hotel?" Luc smoothed his hand over her backside. "The very best part, too," he murmured, kissing her hair and trailing a finger over her face.

"Don't be silly. I'm not the owner. I'm married to the owner." Misty sighed. "Could we really stay one more day?"

"Yes. I'll make a few calls." He lifted her chin. "You *are* part owner of the hotel, darling. I arranged for quite a few properties to be put in your name."

"Take them out of my name, Luc." Misty leaned back, her hands braced against his chest. "I really would rather not own anything. I can always work and—"

"Mystique," Luc interrupted her firmly. His face was grim though his voice was soothing as he added, "I don't give a damn what you do with your money and property, but it's yours and it will stay yours until you sell it or give it away."

Misty laid her head on the sinewy comfort of his chest. "I'm not the rich type," she muttered, kissing a flattened nipple.

"We're never going to get out of this bed and go to dinner if you do that," Luc warned. He shifted her to one side so that they were lying face to face. "But I do like it."

"I like to do it." Misty kissed him again.

In moments they were flesh to flesh, locked in another journey through the dynamic world of love.

A long while later they finally left the bed and began to dress. Misty paused in putting on silky, flesh-colored briefs and turned to catch Luc's gaze on her. She grinned. "I thought I felt someone looking at me."

"Your husband was looking at you, Mrs. Harrison." He let out a long breath. "And if I don't get dressed in the bathroom, we'll never get out of here." When she chuckled, he grimaced at her.

At last they left the cottage and strolled hand in hand to the main lodge.

Dinner was a gourmet's delight, much to Misty's surprise. "Sweetbreads en brioche in the mountains!" she exclaimed. "And prawns Pernod!" She took another bite of the succulent shellfish broiled in lemon and rosemary with a touch of dill. "Isn't that just like you to find a place in the middle of nowhere that serves gourmet food."

"Now that you're a Harrison you'll have all the benefits the family enjoys."

"I'm a Harrison," Misty mused, testing the words.

"Yes, you are, wife. For the next eighty years." Luc lifted a forkful of his boiled lobster for her to taste. "Good?"

Misty nodded. "Yummy."

"Yummy?" Luc laughed. "I like the word. You're a yummy wife."

After they finished glasses of cognac and sampled assorted cheeses, they danced. "Why do I get the feeling that my wife doesn't like cognac?" Luc murmured as they turned and swayed to the slow rhythm of the music.

"It's terribly strong stuff, isn't it?" Misty said, her mind on Luc, not the cognac. "I imagine you could get roaring drunk on it."

"Ummm," he agreed. "But not on the amount you drank, love. I've put down a good bit of it a time or two, and the next day I felt as if the dentist was drilling my teeth through the back of my skull."

Misty lifted her head from his shoulder to look at him and smile. "Dopey."

"Yes." He kissed her nose.

They danced for a while longer, then went back to their room to make love again. The next day they skied all day. Luc never left Misty's side. After dinner that evening they packed and began the drive back to New York.

Misty had the sinking feeling that the paradise they had shared at the Sweetgum Inn was coming to an end.

CHAPTER SIX

Luc HEADED STRAIGHT for his house. "I think Alice may have brought the girls back today," he told Misty.

"Shouldn't we stop at my place and pick up some of my clothes?"

"I think what you'll find in our room will be adequate until we get your clothes tomorrow." Luc grinned at her.

"Luc, tomorrow I won't have a car to carry them in. And you'll be at work."

"Do you have a driver's license?"

"Yes, I learned to drive Uncle Charlie's truck when I was sixteen. But I won't have a car." She was still trying to persuade him to turn back to her apartment when he drove into the garage under his brownstone.

"There." He pointed through the windshield. "That's yours—all gassed and checked and ready to go. There are two sets of keys in our bedroom upstairs, and"—he fumbled on his key chain—"another set right here. I also made another key to the Rolls in case you want to drive it."

"Never," Misty said faintly, her eyes glued to the pale

green Lotus he'd pointed to. "Can we look at it?" she whispered.

"Yes," Luc whispered back, teasing her and kissing her ear.

"You're spoiling me," Misty said with a gulp. "Please don't buy me anything else. I mustn't forget how it is to work for things. If I have to take care of myself again—"

"I'll be taking care of you for the rest of your life," Luc declared. He got out of the car and came around to open her door. His face was taut, and his eyes slid uneasily away from her.

"Luc, please. I didn't mean to hurt your feelings. The car is so beautiful."

He glanced down at her and sighed. "I know. I guess I'm a little too sensitive but I don't like you talking about being away from me, being on your own."

"I won't do it again."

They walked hand and hand over to the sleek car. Misty wouldn't let Luc unlock it until she'd walked all around it and studied each piece of chrome and pale green steel. "It's not quite the color of your eyes, but almost." Luc grinned at her over the top of the roof.

"It's beautiful. I hope I'll know how to drive it."

"Let's find out." He opened the passenger door and climbed inside, reaching over to unlock the driver's door. "Get in, Mystique."

"But, Luc, the luggage. We just got home." She bent down to look at him through the window and bit her lower lip when her eyes encountered his steady gaze. She nodded and sank down into the leather driver's seat. "Nice," she whispered, accepting the keys Luc handed her. She took a deep breath and inserted the key into the ignition. The engine fired with a low growl. Misty took another deep breath and shifted into reverse.

"I thought you might prefer a standard shift to automatic," Luc said, lounging back in his seat, watching her.

"Yes, I do. I just hope I won't strip the gears." She checked the rearview mirror and backed out with scarcely a jerk. She swallowed with nervousness as she turned the car toward the ramp that led to the street. "Here goes," she called with forced brightness.

"Don't worry, darling. Even if you dent it, it can be fixed."

"Luc! Don't say that." Misty turned left at the corner and cruised down Fifth Avenue along the east side of Central Park.

"For someone who hasn't driven in a few years, you're doing fine," Luc said. "I'm proud of you. The only thing I ask is that you never park in a dangerous neighborhood. Use a chauffeur when you go anyplace that might be risky. Promise."

"But, Luc . . . Oh, all right, I promise."

They returned to the underground garage. Misty felt exhilarated at having driven the sophisticated machine.

"That was fun," she told Luc once she'd parked the Lotus and they'd begun to unload the Ferrari. "My sisters will be wild about it."

Luc laughed as he retrieved two large pieces of luggage and gestured to her to take the two smaller ones. "The key with the gold cross on it is the house key."

Misty unlocked the door and preceded him to the basement. While they were still in the dark, she said, "Luc, thank you for the lovely honeymoon. It was wonderful."

He pressed the switch with his elbow, lighting their way, his eyes finding her at once. "It was great for me, too, darling. But we'll have a longer honeymoon in a few months. How would you like to go to Jamaica? A friend of mine has a place there."

"It sounds wonderful, but can you get so much time off?"

"A man is entitled to a honeymoon," Luc insisted.

"How many, do you think?" Misty laughed as she stepped into the hall, glad to set down the two small bags.

"As many as we want." Luc set down his cases with a sigh and kissed her nose. "What do you say we raid the freezer and see if there's a casserole? While it defrosts in the oven, we'll unpack, shower, and change."

"Good thinking." Misty felt her heart turn over when he took her hand to lead her into the kitchen, but she stopped short when Bruno padded down the hall to greet them. "Hello, Bruno," she whispered tremulously, though she felt nervous delight when the dog wagged his short tail and rubbed his muzzle against her hip.

"You've made another conquest." Luc chuckled and kissed her hair.

A note on the counter from Mrs. Wheaton informed them that a casserole was in the refrigerator, needing only to be warmed, and that there were homemade rolls and a pie in separate containers.

"We'll have a feast," Misty said, pulling out the covered dishes. "Ummm, nice salad."

An hour later they finished their meal as strains of Rachmaninoff came from the stereo. Arms around each other, they went upstairs to bed in a sensual, languid eagerness to make love again, which they did all night long.

When the phone rang very early the next morning, Misty grumbled and didn't open her eyes as Luc got out of bed to answer it. "Hello? Alice? Yes, how are the girls? Yes, we had a wonderful time at Sweetgum. We're going back to ski later this winter." He glanced warmly at Misty and smiled. Then the smile left his face, and his brows came together over his eyes. "What? When did this happen? Yes, all right, keep the girls with you until then. Yes, we'll see you tomorrow. John is coming with you? There's no need for that. All right."

Misty stared at Luc as he hung up the phone. He hit his fist lightly against the wall several times and stared at the small print of the French wallpaper. Finally he turned back to Misty. "It seems your father called. He's in town."

"My father?" Immediately she felt as if all the blood had left her body. She wet suddenly dry lips. "Why?"

"He didn't say. He spoke to Aileen. She called Alice." He sat down on the edge of the bed and turned to face her. "Apparently your sisters became very quiet and withdrawn when Alice told them your father was here. So she decided to keep them with her and have Aileen tell your father to call tomorrow. I'll call Aileen and tell her to send your father here."

"I . . . I don't know what I'll do if he tries to take them," Misty said, more to herself than to Luc.

"Darling, it's as much my problem now as yours. Together we'll handle your father and your sisters." Luc held her cold hands in his and stared into her eyes. "No one is going to hurt you again, or bother your sisters. I intend to see to that. You are not to worry about anything."

"But you don't know him," Misty almost whispered. "And you don't know me. I've never told you."

"Darling, were you a victim of incest?"

Misty jumped and started to shake. "No," she said honestly, embarrassed. "My father never touched me . . . not in any way."

Luc stood up, pulling her to her feet and slipping her arms into a robe, then pulling on one himself. "It hurts you so much." He clenched his teeth. "Do you want to talk about it now?"

"No," Misty said. "I want you to hold me."

"That I will gladly do, my love."

Misty held on to him as if for dear life. *I will be strong, I will be strong,* she repeated silently over and over again. *I will not let father do that to me again. I won't.*

"Mystique." Luc's voice sounded harsh. "Stop thinking about it. You have nothing to fear from anyone."

Misty pushed away from him and looked up into his face, which was twisted with concern. "I'm not afraid," she said, letting her head fall back against his chest. But deep inside she knew that wasn't true. She did fear something—that Luc would want to leave her when she told him the terrible story of her life. And she didn't think she could live without him now.

"Your eyes are talking to me, darling," he whispered. "Tell me what you're thinking."

"If you have time before you go to work, I would like to tell you something."

"I'm not going to the bank today."

"You'll be fired for malingering," she said in a feeble effort to lighten the mood.

"I'll find work," he assured her, threading his hand through hers and leading her to the dining room. He smiled at his housekeeper, who was putting a pot of coffee on the table. "We'll serve ourselves, Mrs. Wheaton," Luc said. "We don't wish to be disturbed unless my sister or a Mrs. Aileen Collins phones."

Luc seated Misty at the round table and opened the drapes

to let in the morning sun. At the sideboard he filled two plates, then brought a pitcher of iced orange juice to the table. "Here we are."

"I'm not hungry," Misty said, wringing her hands nervously under the table. "I want to tell you this before I lose my courage."

"All right." Luc sat down beside her, inching his chair close to hers. His eyes held hers. "But first, remember that nothing you say is going to shake our marriage." He lifted her hand to his mouth, kissing each finger and sucking gently on her thumb.

"Luc, you don't know." Misty tried to free her hand, but his grip tightened.

"Tell me."

She let out a long, shuddering sigh and looked out the window to the snowy terrace. "My parents are close to each other. As you know, I'm the oldest. I remember being happy as a small child, but the older I got the more they seemed to turn away from me. By the time I was a teenager my father was finding fault with everything I did. I couldn't please my mother either. From the time I was thirteen, I knew they didn't want me. Each day my mother would recite a list of my deficiencies to my father, and he would rant and rail at me, telling me how I'd failed them, how I wasn't what they wanted, how troublesome I was." Misty swallowed. "Neither one of them ever hit me, but they never hugged me either." She shot a quick look at Luc, then turned back to the window, unable to meet his eyes. "I remember thinking that it was strange they'd had children when they disliked them so much. But as my other sisters grew up, it didn't seem so bad for them. I began to think that it was only me my parents hated, not the others. I was absolutely sure I had failed them, but I didn't know how. I saw a therapist when I came to New York. He taught me not to hate myself."

"You're beautiful," Luc said huskily.

Misty felt a smile tremble on her lips, then disappear. "I used to work so hard to get A's in school. But when I brought my report card home, my father would accuse me of having cheated." She paused but didn't look at Luc. "I had started taking piano lessons when I was seven, but my parents stopped paying for them when I got older. They even sold our piano. After that, I took free lessons at school. I got a job cleaning classrooms after school for a few dollars and the right to practice on the piano in the music room. I liked sports and was on the swim team. But neither of my parents ever came to see me compete, even though I was written up in the newspapers for setting three county records."

Misty's voice faltered, her eyes stinging and her throat going dry. "Then, when I was sixteen, I was asked to the senior prom." Her voice dropped. "My aunt made my dress. I had fun. We went out for breakfast. We came home at six in the morning. My father met me on the front porch. He . . . he called me a whore right in front of my date, Howie Breston. Howie was shocked, but he tried to explain that we'd been with other people the whole time. My father . . . my father said that if I was pregnant, Howie's father would have to pay for the abortion. It wasn't true, Luc. I was a virgin." Misty forced herself to say the words. "After that, I went to live with my aunt and uncle because my father said he wouldn't have a whore in his house. But I'd never . . . never . . ." Misty raised a hand to her trembling mouth. "When I didn't have a baby, my father said that I had gotten rid of it."

"I'll kill him." Luc's harsh voice penetrated her pain-filled thoughts.

"No." She took in a deep breath. "I honestly didn't think it would be so bad for my sisters. Otherwise I would have tried to do something. I really thought it was just me."

"Your parents needed other targets after you left," Luc told her.

"My mother never said very much." Misty shrugged and gave a crooked smile. "But she wasn't much help either."

"No?" Luc kissed each of her palms. "So you went to school while you were living with your aunt and uncle."

"Yes. I got a scholarship to attend the Eastman School of Music. I considered myself lucky to be studying piano." She looked up at Luc. "That's where I met Richard Lentz. We came to New York together."

"I already know all I want to about Richard and Leonard," he said mildly, running a finger down her nose. "As long as I'm the man in your life now, they aren't important."

"I realize now that they never were." Misty wanted to tell Luc what his coming into her life had meant to her, but she couldn't seem to find the words.

Luc remained by her side for the rest of the day. Misty knew it would have been a nightmare without him. That evening she talked to her sisters on the phone. They seemed fine.

The next day Luc rose with her, showered, and dressed. He insisted that she sit down and have a good breakfast. They were finishing their coffee when the phone rang. Mrs. Wheaton brought the phone to the table.

"Yes, Aileen," said Luc. "No, that's fine. In about twenty minutes? Thanks. I'll call my sister." He hung up and dialed. "Alice? Yes. In about twenty minutes. Fine."

Luc gazed at Misty. "I'm sure you know what's going on. We'll entertain your parents in the living room. I'll have Mrs. Wheaton make more coffee. Don't worry, love. I'll be right beside you."

Luc's smile warmed her. "Yes, I know you will," she murmured. "I'm not afraid, not now." And she wasn't. She felt as if a great weight was being lifted from her shoulders. She felt lighter, freer. "You did it," she murmured to her husband as he took her hand and walked with her down the hall to the living room.

"What did I do?" he asked, slipping his arm around her waist.

"Saved my life." She leaned her head on his shoulder. "No matter what happens now, I know I can face it. I'll be strong."

"You *have* been strong, every step of the way. The only thing you've lacked is an appreciation of your own courage."

"And you gave me that." Misty wanted both to laugh out loud and to cry. "You've given me a great deal."

Luc left her for a moment a while later to put a match to the tinder under the fresh logs in the fireplace. He was coming back to her, a now familiar glint in his eye, when the doorbell chimed.

Misty was aware that Luc saw her start, but he just squeezed her hand, saying nothing. She heard him tell the housekeeper that he would answer the door himself.

The murmur of voices came closer. Misty stood facing the door, her hands clasped in front of her as her mother and father entered. Her mother's hair was pulled back in a stiff knot, and she wore a plain dress. Her father was of about the same medium height with freckled skin and thinning sandy hair. His eyes were green; her mother's were pale blue. Both of them were tight-lipped and tense.

Misty was surprised that they looked so small. How alike they were—pinched, stiff, narrow-eyed. "Mother, Father, how are you?" she said.

"Much you ever cared—" her father began.

"Unless you would like to be thrown through that window into the street, you will speak politely to my wife," Luc informed them casually as he closed the door.

"Hey!" Alvan Carver said, his eyes shooting from Misty to his wife to Luc.

"I mean what I say," Luc added, each syllable ringing with conviction in the high-ceilinged room.

"It would seem that Misty has married a bad-mannered person. She isn't like us," her mother pronounced in low tones.

"Neither Misty nor I wish to be discourteous," Luc said formally. "Perhaps you would like to be seated." He gestured toward some chairs near the fireplace.

"Alvan, ask him where the girls are. We can't stay long." Marilyn Carver swallowed, and her eyes became mere slits in her face.

"Yes, we've come to fetch our daughters and take them home," Misty's father declared. But his eyes slid away from her face.

"I don't think they'll be going," Misty said coolly. "But in any case I think they should be allowed to make that decision for themselves."

"You be careful what—" Alvan Carver glanced at Luc and coughed nervously. "We have a right to take our girls home."

"They're of age. They can decide for themselves," Luc said bluntly.

Just then Bruno padded into the room, the irritated voices bringing his ears forward. He went straight to Misty's side and put his muzzle into her hand.

"You hate dogs," her mother grated, her eyes fixed on the animal. "He'll bite you."

Misty stared at her mother with sudden insight. She was a bitter woman, filled with fear and anger. But Misty's own pain was gone. With deep gratitude for her therapist and, most of all, for Luc, she realized that she no longer hated her parents.

She looked at Luc, trying to convey all the love she felt for him. Her world seemed complete.

In the silence that followed, the doorbell chimed again, and Alice and John entered, followed by Misty's sisters. Alice launched immediately into angry speech. "I don't know what the trouble is, but my lawyer, Willard Harter of Harter, Harter and Young, will join us here this morning if we need him. And he tells me that Mr. and Mrs. Carver don't have a leg to stand on." Alice placed her arm in front of the three Carver girls like a protective barrier. Misty's sisters looked wary but unafraid.

Misty watched Betsy bite her lip, then lift her chin, and she felt her own face break into a tentative smile. She glanced at Celia, who nodded and gave Misty a shaky smile. Marcy shrugged, and kept a sharp eye on her parents.

"Girls," their mother greeted them, pursing her lips.

Misty's sisters nodded warily in greeting.

Alvan Carver nodded, too, puzzlement flashing momentarily in his eyes.

"Darling, this is Alice's husband, John." Luc indicated a tall, rather stoop-shouldered man to Misty's right.

"I'm also backup for Alice," John explained *sotto voce*. "She's fully committed to your sisters." His eyes glinted with amusement. "I'm going to try to prevent her from running your parents out of the country."

Misty felt a knot of tears in her throat as John patted her shoulder and went to stand next to her sisters. Why had she been worried? Hadn't Luc told her he would take care of everything? She stayed in the comfort of her husband's arm as she faced her parents. "The girls will be staying with us, Father. Marcy and Celia want to go to school, and Betsy may decide she wants to go, too. They'll make their own choices."

Misty's mother was struggling visibly with her anger.

"You know what you are," she said threateningly. "I'm too much a lady to use the word, but you know what you are." Her mother's sharp eyes darted to each sister in turn. "All you wanted to do was chase the boys. You didn't want to stay home with me and learn to cook and sew as I did when I was a girl. None of you is like me."

"How dare you speak to your own daughters like that!" Alice shot at her. "You will not be allowed to intimidate them." She looked down her nose at Misty's mother.

"Intimidate them!" Alvan echoed. "We're their parents. We've come to take them home."

"We won't go, Daddy," Celia said. "We want to live here and go to school."

Misty's mother turned red. "How dare you! Alvan, listen to what they're saying. Do something." She whirled on Misty. "You were never pretty! Never! You were an ugly child, and so were they. They never—" Abruptly she stopped herself. She looked around at the people staring at her. "We . . . we have come to take our girls home with us. The neighbors—"

"They aren't going, Mother," Misty said in a quiet voice, feeling a rush of pity for her mother and her bewildered father. "Perhaps someday they'll want to see you, but not for a while." She gestured for her sisters to come toward her. "They're staying here."

"At our house," John said mildly, taking a pipe out of his pocket and putting it in his mouth. "Alice has already registered them at a small college near our home. If after a time they choose to do something else . . ." He shrugged, smiling owlishly at Misty's parents.

As Misty's father looked at each of his daughters in turn, he seemed to age ten years right before their eyes.

"I think that settles it, then." Luc turned as Mrs. Wheaton pushed a coffee cart into the room. "Ah, I'd love a cup. I'll fix you one, darling. Betsy, will you pour for our guests?"

Misty felt deeply sorry for her parents. But she felt no rancor, no bitterness. Luc had freed her of those destructive emotions. The heavy weight she'd carried for years was gone. She was finally at peace with herself.

"Coffee, Mother? Father?" Betsy quizzed, smiling as she took charge of the refreshments.

"I think we'll leave," Alvan Carver said flatly. Again he looked at each of his four daughters. Then he took his wife's arm, and they walked to the door.

"I'll see you out." Misty followed them, Luc at her side. She took a deep breath at the touch of his warm hand at her waist. "Mother, Father, you're free to visit any of us at any time. Just call first." Her voice was low and sure.

"My wife and I will welcome you to our home," Luc said formally. "And of course you may see your other daughters, in either my presence or in my wife's."

"I see." Her father's face had taken on a gray cast. "I think maybe we might see you someday, girl." He glanced at his thin-lipped wife. "Come along, Marilyn. I'll take you home."

Her mother scarcely looked at Misty before she clutched her husband's arm. "Let's go."

"Father . . ." Misty took his arm, the first physical contact she'd had with him in many years. "I want you to know that I truly believe it's never too late to start over in life."

Without meeting her eyes he nodded, then walked through the door with his wife. Misty watched them as they got into their car and drove away.

"Are you all right, love?" Luc asked her.

"Yes, I'm fine. I feel so sorry for them—for my father—for all of us really. It all seems very sad." She looked up at him. "But you've given me hope." She pressed his arm. "I saw them with new eyes today."

Luc shrugged. "Your mother needs counseling. So does your father. Maybe they'll begin to realize that."

"Luc, I want to keep in touch with my father and see that my mother gets the help she needs." She turned to face him. "But I never would have seen any of this without you. I would have kept all that insecurity to myself forever." She smiled at him.

Luc kissed her nose. "You hid too much of your pain, my love. Especially from your parents. But you've come a long way since you lived with them. Even before I met you, you were well on the way to coming to terms with yourself. When you left Richard and Leonard, you were already beginning to question your reasons for doing things."

"I swore off all men."

"Lord, what a close call I had," Luc teased, kissing her lightly.

They walked back to the living room, where Alice announced, "Lucas, the girls have decided to come with me. They'll be starting school soon, and there will be riding and music lessons and of course we must begin to prepare them for their debut."

"Debut?" the three girls and Misty said in unison.

Luc looked accusingly at his brother-in-law. "Don't glare at me, Luc," John said mildly, returning his pipe to his pocket when his wife gave him a long-suffering look.

"A debut isn't necessary," Misty began.

"Don't be silly, Mystique, dear," Alice said. "And you mustn't worry about the money. Lucas has scads of money, and I intend to bill him for everything." Alice smiled, unrepentant.

"Of course," Luc agreed dryly. "But the fuss is what I hate. I'll be damned if I'll wear white tie and tails to a debutante cotillion. It isn't necessary," he told his sister.

"How like you to act the village idiot, Lucas," Alice commented. "Well, if you don't wear tails, you shall be the only one who does not." She rolled her eyes at Misty, who smiled back weakly. "How can you think of shaming your new wife that way?"

Betsy giggled. "Misty's not ashamed of Luc. Are you, Misty?"

"No, of course not."

"Well of course she's not ashamed now, but think how she'll feel when you arrive at the club without any clothes on."

"I could put a jewel in my navel," Luc offered.

"Fig leaf would be better," John said, then coughed behind his hand.

"Come, girls, this is getting us nowhere. We have to get you some clothes. We'll go to Saks. We'll get your shoes at Lord and Taylor. I like their shoes." Alice's voice floated behind her as she urged the girls to kiss Misty good-bye and herded them into the foyer.

"John," Luc said in a warning tone.

John held up his hand, palm out. "Don't start with me, Luc. She's your sister. Besides, I wouldn't interfere if I could. Alice is having a marvelous time. She's sunny in the morning, and she greets me at the door in the evening with a smile."

"What? No rose in her teeth and martini in her hand?" Luc teased, reaching out to pull Misty to his side.

"Ummm? Not a bad idea. I'll suggest it while I'm following the group through Saks. I relish the thought that all the bills will be going directly to you."

"Pirate," Luc accused mildly as he and Misty followed John to the front door. "Don't forget that they'll need recreational clothes, not just ball gowns."

"I'm sure Alice has a list." John laughed and closed the door after himself.

Misty turned at once to confront Luc. "Wait until we're back in the living room, darling," he said. "You can ring for more coffee before you berate me." He chuckled and chucked her under the chin.

"Luc, it isn't funny! You can't let Alice run up big bills for my sisters. They have enough clothes." Misty bit her lip.

"Would you mind buying wardrobes for them if you had the money to do it?" He sat down on the couch and pulled her into his lap, cuddling her close.

"Stop. Mrs. Wheaton will come in any minute." She pushed against him, laughing. "And, no, of course I wouldn't mind buying clothes for my sisters." She paused as he chuckled. "You tricked me," she accused, pulling gently on his hair.

"Maybe a little. The point is, darling, we're well able to pay for any number of wardrobes Alice thinks necessary. If you like, I'll arrange for your accountant to pay the bills instead of mine."

"I have an accountant?" Misty asked, her voice faint.

"Of course. A very good man from the same firm the family has always used. You won't mind that, will you?"

"Huh? No, I guess not. Oh, here comes Mrs. Wheaton." Misty's voice failed as the older woman entered carrying a silver coffeepot, which she put on the serving cart. She smiled at Misty and Luc.

Misty wriggled on Luc's lap, feeling embarrassed, but

he held her still with a minimum of effort. "Darling," he whispered in her ear as the housekeeper replenished the cream and sugar, "you're arousing me."

"Eeek!" Misty squeaked. "Stop that!" she hissed, giving Mrs. Wheaton a weak smile when the older woman looked up in query. "Ah, nice weather we're having," Misty said.

Mrs. Wheaton looked momentarily puzzled. "There's a travelers' warning out, and the snow has turned to sleet, but I guess you like cold weather, don't you, Mrs. Harrison?" Mrs. Wheaton lifted the empty silver pot and left the room.

"Yes, you do like cold weather, don't you, Mrs. Harrison?" Luc teased, burying his nose in her neck. "In fact, the next time we go to Sweetgum, I'm going to make love to you in the snow."

"You'll be arrested," Misty said, trying not to laugh. "You're much too sure of yourself."

"I'm sure of the way I feel about you." He settled her more comfortably on his lap. "Now, I talked to Mother this morning, and she's inviting us over on Saturday to introduce the new Mrs. Harrison to some friends. I told her I thought we could make it, but that I had to check with you first."

Misty stiffened. "How many friends?"

"Just a few. She doesn't like to seat more than thirty in her dining room, even though she has room for sixty."

"Thirty? Sixty? Oh, my goodness," Misty groaned.

"If being the guest of honor bothers you, I'll tell Mother we can't come."

"We can't do that to your mother." Misty raised her head from his chest. "Doesn't your family ever do anything on a small scale?"

"I guess not," Luc said thoughtfully.

She tightened her arms around his neck. "Luc, it rather frightened me that my sisters made no move to kiss my parents, or express a wish to go with them. It makes me think I've been blind all these years not to have seen that they were going through the same thing I did."

"I don't think they suffered as much as you did. Truly, honey, I mean that. The three of them are close in age, so they could support one another, while you, being considerably older, had to face it on your own. I watched your sisters while your parents were here. I saw the same pity in their faces that I saw on yours, but not the same anxiety."

"Oh, Luc." Misty sobbed into his neck.

He held her for long minutes, comforting her. Then he stood and pulled her up to face him. "Now we're going to change and go to see a designer I know."

"One that you used with your mistresses, you mean," Misty teased. She punched his arm, feeling buoyant with happiness because she was with Luc.

"Mrs. Harrison! I'm shocked," he exclaimed with mock indignation. "Insinuating such a thing about your husband." He cupped his hands on her bent elbows, and hoisted her up his body until they were mouth to mouth. "Shame on you," he whispered against her lips. "My feelings are hurt. Kiss me and make it better."

"You fool." Misty's laughter faded as his mouth claimed hers. They kissed deeply, their mouths moving on each other as though they were seeking the secret of life.

Luc pulled away first, breathing hard. "Lord, wife, we'd better go now, or we'll be up the stairs and in bed before you know it." He let her slide down his body.

"So? Who's arguing?" Misty stretched up and licked the corner of his mouth.

His face flushed, his eyes narrowing on her. He placed his palms on either side of her face. "Siren," he whispered. "Yes."

"When we come home, we're going to have a nice, leisurely soak in a hot tub, then—"

"Let's do it now," Misty urged.

"No. You're just trying to turn me away from my objective."

"But, Luc, Morey designs all my clothes. I like his work."

Luc regarded her for long minutes. "All right. But let's just see if Charine has anything that would suit you. Then we'll drive to Morey's place and take a look."

Misty nodded. "But please don't buy me too much. I'd like to give some of what I have to the poor." She paused, watching him. "I . . . I can use the money I earn at the Terrace—ah, I know you give to many charities . . ."

"Darling, I'll write out a check to any organization you

name." He shook his head. "Just when I think I have you figured out, you show another unexpected facet of yourself."

They freshened up, changed their clothes, and went down to the garage after Mrs. Wheaton informed them that Melton had arrived.

"I asked the chauffeur for the Rolls to come over today," Luc explained. "I thought it would be easier if we didn't have to fight traffic." He held open the door for her, nodding a greeting to Melton. "Comfortable?" Luc asked Misty.

"Luc . . ." Misty had pressed a switch that opened up a small bar with a desk and a telephone. "A person could practically live in here!"

"Great place for a seduction." He grinned when she glared at him. "No, I have never seduced a woman in the back seat of the Rolls. Would you like to be the first?"

"Yes." She laughed when his mouth dropped open. It delighted her to catch him off guard for once. He was always taking her by surprise.

"Next time I'll drive the Rolls, we'll park it someplace, and we'll see what we can do," Luc promised.

"Not in the middle of Manhattan!"

"And why not?" he teased.

They were still bantering when the sleek vehicle pulled up in front of a posh shop on Madison Avenue.

"It looks very expensive," Misty said as they got out. She watched over her shoulder as the Rolls merged into traffic.

"Just take a look at a few things," Luc urged. "We won't buy much. We can get most of your things at Morey's. In fact, how about suggesting to Alice that he make your sisters' debutante dresses? Alice would be bound to tell her friends about Morey." Luc shrugged as they approached a glass door bearing the name Charine in gold scrollwork. "Come on, darling."

The salon was lavishly decorated in cream and turquoise colors. Misty was a little nervous. She didn't feel comfortable in places like this, where the salespeople were often patronizing. Although she had learned to handle that sort of behavior at the Terrace Hotel, she preferred to avoid such places.

A tall woman with black hair in a French twist and

wearing a beige silk dress came toward them, smiling. "Mr. Harrison, how nice to see you. I'm afraid Charine isn't here today, but may I help with something?"

"Hello, Lois." Luc smiled. He spoke quietly to the woman, and she nodded agreeably and walked toward the back of the shop.

Misty felt as if she'd just received a hard blow. Unreasoning anger and jealousy swept over her because her husband had just smiled at the woman. She sucked her breath in sharply, trying to control her irrational emotions.

"Darling? What is it?" Luc bent over her.

"I'm going to sock her if she smiles at you again. How did you know her name? How many women have you brought here?" The questions tumbled from Misty's mouth. She pressed her lips together in an effort to stop them. Luc grinned, and her temper flared. "And don't you dare laugh, Lucas Harrison," she fumed, which made him laugh out loud. Just then Lois and another woman arrived carrying several dresses over their arms.

Still chuckling, Luc turned to face them. "Would it be possible for someone to model them for my wife?"

Lois looked momentarily overcome by surprise. "Your wife? Well, congratulations, Mr. Harrison. I didn't see an announcement in the paper."

"No doubt it will appear this week sometime."

Lois nodded. "Won't you both follow me?" She led them into an inner room with several Louis Quinze chairs arranged in a semicircle in front of a tiny stage one step up from the floor. In minutes the curtains parted, and a model glided forward wearing a low-cut flame-colored dress.

Luc frowned. "That's not your color."

Misty was about to agree when the model turned, and the color took on more cherry tones. "It might suit me," she mused.

"I don't want anything to detract from the color of your hair," Luc said, reaching up to wrap a strand around his finger.

Dresses, suits, and coats followed in quick succession, but Misty's thoughts kept returning to the first dress she'd seen. When the women finished showing her the garments, she asked to try on the red dress.

It fit perfectly. Misty stared at herself in the three-way mirror in the dressing room. "You were right, Mrs. Harrison," said Lois. "That dress suits you wonderfully. It emphasizes your glorious hair."

Misty looked down at the dress. "I'd like to show it to my husband, please."

The medium-heeled black pumps she was wearing didn't look quite right with the knee-length silk chiffon that wafted about her like scarlet flames. The many-tiered skirt was cut on the bias with a ruffle that went from breast to hem, delineating her every curve.

Luc was lounging in a chair talking to a salesclerk next to him. When he saw Misty he rose at once. "Darling, you were right. That dress is sensational on you. We'll take it, Lois. And I want all the accessories." He leaned down to kiss Misty, his smile wide, his eyes hot. "Are you sure there's nothing else you'd like to try on while you're here?"

"No, thank you, Luc. This dress is all I could possibly want."

He nodded and kissed her. Misty watched as he signed the bill, chatting with Lois, who stood at his shoulder laughing. Misty's temper rose.

When they stepped out into the crisp January day, she took hold of her husband's arm. "I don't know what you ever were to that woman, but I do know she has designs on you."

Luc looked down at her in amazement. "She didn't have a chance before I met you. She has a lot less chance now."

Misty let out a sigh of relief. She was beaming up at him as Melton pulled up to the curb in the Rolls. But Luc didn't seem to notice that their driver had arrived. He was taking her into his arms, his eyes alight with passion.

"Luc!" Misty stared up at him, perplexed by his determined expression. "Melton is here."

"What? Oh, yes. Let's go." He ushered her into the car and climbed in after her, keeping her close to his side as he reached into his breast pocket and brought out a jeweler's case with the name Cartier's inside the lid.

"A diamond pendant!" Misty exclaimed. "Oh, Luc, it's too much."

"I think this necklace will go very nicely with that new

dress. I bought it when I had your engagement stone reset."
His lazy grin widened as she gasped in astonishment.

"A necklace and earrings and two rings," she whispered,
studying the diamond pendant.

"The emerald in your engagement ring isn't new. It belonged to my Grandmother Stuyvesant. I purchased the other
items right after Christmas when I decided that you were
going to be very special to me. Do you think the pendant
will go nicely with your new dress?"

"I think it would look exquisite with a washcloth," she
muttered.

"Mystique, what a great idea! Tonight after dinner I want
you to wear your diamond and a washcloth."

Misty laughed and snuggled closer to him. When he
gasped she looked up at him. "What's wrong?"

"Nothing. I've just discovered what my favorite thing
is." Luc kissed her hard, forestalling further any questions.
"It's your wonderful laugh, my sweet."

CHAPTER SEVEN

MARRIED LIFE WAS EXCITING! At least Misty found it so. She was contemplating the thought as she bent over the keyboard in the Edwardian Room of the Terrace Hotel. She smiled to herself as she thought of Luc and how he would be coming soon to pick her up. He'd take her home . . . and make love to her. Imagining it sent a tremor of excitement through her, and she hit two keys at once with her middle finger. Don't think of Luc while you're playing, she chided herself, forcing herself to concentrate on the music.

But in moments her thoughts had slipped back to Luc. He held her continually in thrall. He had merged her life completely with his. They had been married for only six weeks, yet Misty could scarcely remember what life had been like without him. She performed only two nights a week now, Tuesdays and Thursdays, and instead of playing until two or three in the morning, she finished at twelve, when Luc arrived to drive her home. Her breath rasped in her throat at the thought of going home with him.

"Hey, Mystique," Willis whispered, "you just played 'My Man' three times in a row."

Misty looked up at Willis, biting her lip. "I have to concentrate better."

"Not that it wasn't nice." Willis winked at her.

She shook her head and gave a half-laugh, half-groan. "No more daydreaming, I promise."

She switched to the Ravel Bolero, welcoming the intricate fingering since it forced her to concentrate on every nuance.

When she looked up sometime later in response to a burst of applause, the first person she saw was her husband. Her face broke into a brilliant smile. She had given up any pretense of acting aloof with him. Although she hadn't said the words "I love you" out loud, she was more committed to Lucas Stuyvesant Harrison than she had ever been to anyone.

She moved her hands on the keyboard in a complicated introduction to one of her favorite love songs, "Something Was Missing," from the musical *Annie*. On impulse she did something that she rarely did; she tilted up the piano mike and sang the lovely words of the melody. Not once as she sang did she take her eyes off Luc.

When she finished several people came up to the piano and made requests. She played the songs they asked to hear, but she didn't sing.

At midnight Luc left his seat and walked up to her. He took her arm and lifted her from the piano bench, keeping his arm around her waist as they walked along the hall to the small dressing room. "Uh-uh, not tonight, angel," he said when she paused. "I had your clothes put in the penthouse suite. You can change there."

"Luc, I thought we went all through that. I don't mind that the—"

"Dressing room is so small. Yes, I know. But I thought we'd stay here tonight and go home in the morning, so I had your clothes moved to our suite."

"Why? I mean, it's just as easy..." Her voice trailed off as she saw the harsh look on his face. "Luc?"

"We've been married for six weeks today. I thought you might want to celebrate," he said stiffly as they stepped into the elevator.

"Oh, I do." Misty slipped her arms around his waist under his jacket. "I didn't think you would remember." She glanced up at him. "I thought men always ignored those things."

"I'm not likely to forget my own marriage." She noted a slight edge to his voice.

The elevator doors opened. Misty kept her arm around him as they walked into their suite. "I didn't mean to hurt your feelings," she said.

Luc loosened her arm from around him and headed toward the bathroom, his back rigid. Misty stood looking at the closed door, then walked over to the windows and stared out at the Manhattan skyline. The bathroom door opened a few minutes later, but she stayed where she was. She sensed Luc's presence close behind her.

"I'm sorry. I was hurt," he murmured. "I didn't think I could ever feel that way—like a child."

She turned slowly and looked up at him. "I know. We still don't know each other well enough not to be sensitive about what we say."

"Smile at me, darling," Luc said huskily.

"You always say that to me." Warmth suffused her face.

Inch by inch he pulled her toward him until they were lightly touching all along their two lengths. "I thought by now you knew that your smile was one of my favorite things."

He nibbled on her throat, trailing a line of tiny bites from one pulse point to the other.

"This happens to be one of *my* favorite things," Misty murmured as Luc's mouth traveled over her bare shoulders. "You nibbling on my skin."

"Another one of mine as well." His answer was muffled as he lifted her up his body with one strong arm. "I want you all the time." He sounded almost fierce as he swung her up into his arms and carried her to their bed. "I like your sisters very much, but I'm glad they've decided to stay with Alice and John most of the time." His voice held both anger and puzzlement as he sat her down on the edge of the bed and removed her shoes, then asked her to stand so that he could pull the long silken dress from her body. "I love my work, but sometimes I can't stand to leave you. You have such power over me." Ironic amusement filled his face.

"I hit a sour note tonight, and I played the same song three times, because I was thinking of you," Misty admitted.

"I know. I was there." He grinned. "You didn't see me. Don't be embarrassed, my love."

Misty loosened the studs on his evening shirt. "Maybe we should tell each other more, not hide so much from each other."

He laid her back on the bed—she was still wearing her silky briefs—and divested himself of his remaining clothes. He was holding the sleeve of his shirt when he looked down at her, his eyes appraising her hotly. "Do you know what you look like at this moment, my child-woman? Your red-gold hair looks like sunlight. Your eyes are like the most precious jade. Your skin is creamy pink. Your breasts are beautiful." His rakish grin almost masked the passion in his eyes. "And you have the cutest bottom in three counties."

"Not four?" Misty teased, thanking the fates that Luc thought her lovely.

"Mrs. Harrison . . ." Luc sat facing her on the bed. "I'd like to talk further with you, but I find that my mind can't hold any thought except how beautiful you are."

"Luc." Misty's body surged forward with a passionate need to love him. She raised her hands to explore his chest, tugging gently on his nipples, her energy building as she saw that he was already aroused.

"I feel I should warn you that I don't have a high tolerance for your loving," he said, his eyes following her hands as she probed, caressed, teased, and touched him.

"Just be patient," she cooed. As his body jerked and bent in response to her every touch, she felt consumed with a thrilling sense of power. "Luc, you're so beautiful." She squeezed the taut muscles of his stomach, then boldly let her hands slide lower and lower until she grasped his manhood, massaging gently.

Luc groaned and reached out to grab her waist. "Much as I love your sensual massage, darling"—he lowered her fully onto the bed and leaned over her— "my restraint just blew apart." In a feverish frenzy his hands and mouth ministered to her.

When he gently parted her thighs to enter her, she was whimpering with desire for him. At once they went up in flames, holding each other, calling out each other's name.

Afterward they kissed good night, their mouths remaining only inches apart as they slept.

Misty woke once in the night with a strange longing. But she was too sleepy to analyze it. Tightening her arms around Luc's waist, she fell back into a deep slumber.

When she woke again, she was alone. She blinked in confusion at the sight of the unfamiliar room, then remembered that they had stayed at the Terrace Hotel suite. "Luc," she called, masking a yawn behind her hand.

"Yes, darling, I'm here. Come and take a shower with me."

Delighted, Misty leaped out of bed and ran unclothed to the bathroom. She paused just inside the door to watch Luc wipe the last traces of shaving cream from his face. "Oh, you're already finished," she said, disappointed. "I like to watch you shave." Her body tingled from the way he was looking at her.

"You do?" He sounded distracted. "From now on I'll call you before I shave." He took a deep breath and pulled her into his arms. "You're too much of a distraction, Mrs. Harrison. Seeing you like this makes me want to cancel my meeting this morning."

"You can't." She gave a breathy laugh. "It's with the board of directors, and you told me last week that it's very important."

"So it is." He sighed, dropping the towel from around his waist and leading her to the shower stall. "I've enjoyed my work since the first day I joined the bank after graduate school, but when I see you naked in front of me, I could chuck the whole thing."

"Don't you dare, Mr. Harrison. You have to support me."

"And the little Harrisons who will be coming along." Luc pulled her forward and began to scrub her back with the loofah sponge.

Misty clutched at him, stunned by what he had said. Children! She couldn't have children! She'd vowed long ago never to have them. What if she turned out to be a terrible mother like her own had been? She shuddered. Why had it never occurred to her that Luc might want children?

"Darling, you're cold. Let me make the water warmer."

"No, no. It's fine." She tried to smile up at him, but when she saw his eyes narrow in concentration on her, she pulled his head down and kissed him deeply. She kept her mouth on his until she felt his lips begin moving against hers, his mouth opening, his tongue thrusting against hers.

As they toweled each other dry and put on their clothes, Misty kept up a ceaseless round of questions concerning the board of directors' meeting.

"You've always been a good listener," Luc drawled, "but you seem obsessed with business this morning." He regarded her speculatively. She shrugged and didn't respond.

Even as they descended in the elevator to the hotel foyer, Misty felt him studying her. Melton was waiting for them outside the front entrance when she and Luc emerged.

Luc pulled her close to him. "We promised to be open with each other," he reminded her in low tones, his eyes piercing hers.

"We are open," she said weakly.

"Then tell me what's on your mind. What's making you frown?"

"Ah . . . I was trying to figure out what music to play on Thursday." As soon as she said the words, he stiffened beside her. He knew she was lying, but he didn't contradict her.

They were silent in the limousine on the way to the bank. Misty's head was filled with worries. How long had it been since she'd been to a gynecologist? When had she had her last menstrual period?

"Luc . . ." She licked suddenly dry lips as the car came to a stop in front of the bank.

"I'll be a little late tonight," he told her.

"Luc, we promised your mother and father we'd go out to the house Friday night and stay the weekend. They're giving another dinner party and—"

"Mystique, I really am in a hurry." Luc kissed her lightly

on the cheek and hurried out of the car. Melton pulled away from the curb, not seeming to notice that his passenger was pressing her fist against her mouth. She was bewildered and upset. She had withdrawn from Luc, and he had sensed the change at once.

Back home, Misty was greeted by Bruno and Mrs. Wheaton. She listened to what the older woman said about preparing dinner, promptly forgot it, and raced up to her bedroom, Bruno at her heels. Nowadays he rarely left her side when she was in the house, and she had come to love the dog.

She dialed her gynecologist's number and made an appointment, feeling frustrated when she had to make it for two weeks away. "Would you put me on a cancellation list, please?" she asked the nurse.

She paced the bedroom rug, back and forth, back and forth. She couldn't have a child. She couldn't take the chance that she would be like her mother. To hurt a child that way! She buried her face in her hands as tears filled her eyes. Bruno whined at her side, and she patted his head. Why had she stopped taking the pill? The headaches they caused weren't so bad! Why had she assumed she wouldn't get pregnant when she went off the pill? She started in surprise when Mrs. Wheaton entered.

"Mrs. Harrison, I knocked, but— Why, what's wrong?" the older woman queried, coming farther into the room.

"It's nothing, Mrs. Wheaton. Just a slight headache, that's all." The housekeeper frowned, but she left when Misty assured her she was fine.

That evening Luc was silent and aloof as they drank coffee after dinner, a silver tray between them. The thought of making love with him worried Misty, but the thought of alienating him was an even greater fear. Nothing must come between them! Hesitantly, she stood up and went over to sit on his lap, cuddling close to him.

At first he did not respond. Then, gradually, his hold on her tightened. "Witch," he whispered into her hair. He began to caress her with slow, seductive strokes. Moments later he surged out of the chair, holding her in his arms, and strode up the stairs, his cheeks flushed with passion.

That night their lovemaking was frenzied. Misty felt as

though they were joined not just in body, but in blood and in spirit as well.

Unlike other nights, when they had cuddled and joked softly for a long time before falling asleep, now they held each other in fierce silence until welcome sleep took them both away.

The days remaining before she and Luc were scheduled to drive to his parents' house on Long Island were fraught with tension. Not all of Misty's efforts succeeded in melting the frost between them.

"It's unfortunate that I love you, husband," she whispered to the framed picture on her dressing room table that Friday afternoon as she packed her clothes for the weekend. "I was a fool not to go back on the pill as soon as we were married, but I got headaches...Maybe Dr. Wagner can suggest an alternative."

Just then Luc came into their bedroom, stripping the tie from his neck. "Since I'm here, why not talk to me instead of to my picture?"

"Ah...I was just asking your image if you would like two pairs of jeans packed or one." Misty watched his relaxed features tighten. *He knows I'm lying,* she moaned to herself.

"I'll pack the rest of my things," Luc told her, striding to the second bathroom attached to their suite.

"Luc," she whispered aloud. She couldn't explain to him how she felt, even though he'd met her mother. He would tell her she was wrong, she supposed, but she couldn't take a chance with their child. What if she was as twisted as her mother? No...no...

Talk between them was sporadic as they finished packing, checked with Mrs. Wheaton, and left the brownstone. "In the time since I've lived in New York, I'd never gone to Long Island until I visited your parents' and Alice's homes," Misty said as they left the city. She cleared her throat. "I enjoyed dining with them last month."

"So you told me." Luc's words were clipped.

"So I did." Misty began to burn from discomfort. "I was only trying to make conversation."

"Yes, you make conversation, but you're not honest with me. Is that how it should be?"

"What are you trying to say?"

"Look, Mystique, I'm not the one who's being evasive."

"I am not an evasive person," she shot back, her temper beginning to let go.

"What you mean is, you're not evasive or dissembling with most people. With your husband you are." His words seemed to echo in the confines of the car.

"Where the hell do you get off telling me what I am or am not, Mr. Perfect!"

"When did I ever do that to you?"

"When didn't you?" she retorted.

"There's no sense in continuing this discussion."

"Don't patronize me," she cried. As Luc pulled off the expressway and headed toward the North Shore, she faced out the window, ignoring the tree-lined avenues, open fields, and glimpses of Long Island Sound.

Silence reigned for what seemed like hours to Misty. Then the car was turning into a curving driveway bordered with rhododendrons, their brown leaves like claws snapping in the cold wind. The denuded trees looked to Misty like phantom guardians of the large sandstone and brick house they were approaching. Situated in the middle of a tremendous expanse of lawn, the building seemed to brood over the barren landscape.

Before Luc had pulled the car to a complete stop under the porte cochere, the double oak doors were flung open, and two boys of five and seven raced down the steps. "Good Lord," Luc muttered with evident amusement. "Attila the Hun and Genghis Khan are here." He turned to Misty, grim humor on his face. "My sister Deirdre's brood has arrived. My two nephews, Greg and James, who are now assaulting my car. Wait a minute, you two, until I get the door open. Their baby sister Jennifer, who has mastered the dubious art of smiling and spitting up at the same time, is also undoubtedly here." Misty gave a tentative laugh as the boys clambered onto the hood of the Ferrari. Wincing, Luc bounded out of the car and tackled them. "All we need now is for Velma to show up with her gaggle from Chicago. Janie, whom you met, is their only civilized child."

"Luc, you cad. Are you trying to kill my angels?" A tall, slender woman with gray eyes and ash blond hair similar to Luc's stood at the top of the steps, dressed in a simple pink cashmere dress. She hurried down as Misty stood uncertainly next to the car. "And you must be Mystique, the beauty who finally corralled the famous Elusive One. Good for you. What did you use? Bear traps?"

"A lasso," Misty answered, watching Luc pluck the two boys from the car and imprison one under each arm. "As a last resort I was planning to use poison—nothing lethal, you understand, just something to slow him down."

Deirdre threw back her head and laughed. "Oh, I love it. He has, indeed, met his match." Not seeming to mind the cold, she held out her hand. "I'm Deirdre. And I still think you *should* consider poison."

"Thank you for the advice." Misty chuckled at the boys, who were making faces at their uncle and smiling at her.

"Very funny," Luc said, panting and red-faced as they all climbed the steps to the open doors. "Stop wriggling, you monsters," he admonished. "Ah, Hawes. Get the bags, will you? Thanks."

"They drive him crazy, but he loves them," Deirdre explained. "How many will you have, do you think? Oh, Lord, Luc, watch them, will you? That's mother's Tang vase."

Misty felt vastly relieved that Deirdre had been momentarily diverted from the question of children.

"Lord, Dee, couldn't you peel one of them off?" asked a tall blond man coming into the massive foyer. He watched as Luc wrestled with the boys on the marble floor, again coming dangerously close to a Louis Quatorze table on which stood a rare vase of roses and baby's breath. He came forward to introduce himself. "I'm Ted Manning, father of the twosome that's assaulting your husband on the floor."

"Hello," Misty said, grinning back. All of Luc's family made her feel so at ease.

"Is that you, Mystique, dear?" Althea, Luc's mother, came out of the mammoth living room carrying a baby girl dressed in a pink pinafore, the one blond curl on top of her head tied with a pink ribbon. "Those are the boys, dear," she explained, casually handing her the baby. "And this is Jennifer. She's very good, but you should have this towel just in case." She adjusted the flannel square on Misty's shoulder.

Deirdre chuckled. "Let me take the baby until you can get your coat off." She hefted the baby onto her hip, and Ted took Misty's coat. "I've just met your sisters, and they're delightful. I like the idea of holding a Mardi Gras party to introduce the girls to society rather than waiting until the fall, don't you?" Deirdre handed Jennifer back to Misty.

"Ah . . ." Misty couldn't remember having heard about a Mardi Gras party.

"What the hell are you talking about?" Luc asked from the floor. Ted told the boys to behave, and Luc managed to shake them off for a moment. "We don't know about any Mardi Gras party. What in the world has Alice been up to?"

"You should see the girls." Deirdre giggled. "They look so preppy in their skirts and sweaters, and they love their schools. They seem very excited about Mardi Gras. Ted and I have decided to fly back for the occasion, and I know Vel and Ken will want to come, too. I understand just everyone will be there—at least three hundred guests."

Misty gasped. Luc stared at his sister in astonishment. "She's lost her mind," he declared.

"McLaren will do the flowers," Deirdre continued, "and Bijou is handling the food, and a couturier by the name of Morey is making all the clothes, including mother's dress." Deirdre finished breezily, apparently unaware that her brother's face had turned brick red.

"Oh, that's lovely. Morey's a friend," Misty offered, then bit her lip as Luc glared at her.

"Do you realize that she's creating a . . . a . . ."

"A bang-up do?" Deirdre suggested sweetly.

"A stampede," Luc corrected angrily. "And you can stop laughing, Ted. You'll be ordered to wear white tie, too."

Luc's brother-in-law chuckled and held up a hand. "Not me. This is your party, right, honey?" He glanced at his wife, who scowled back at him. "Now, Dee, surely you don't intend for me to—".

"Are you going to be the only one who lets those lovely girls down?" Deirdre demanded, seeming to swell with indignation.

"Yes, will you be a cad?" Luc quizzed.

"Quiet, Lucas." Ted shot his now chuckling brother-in-law a dirty look. "Dee, listen to me. Boys, quiet down. Dee . . ." His voice trailed off as he followed his wife back into the living room.

"Come inside and have some tea, dear," Luc's mother offered serenely. "We're just having a quiet evening at home. Hildebrand and George have joined us, but no one else will come until tomorrow night." She smiled at Misty and took her arm.

"You invited those bores?" Luc demanded.

"That is an unkind way to speak of your cousins," his mother admonished as she led Misty into the living room, which seemed to be filled with people, all of them talking loudly and gesturing wildly.

Ted was still pleading with Deirdre, who was talking to John and flapping her hand at Ted. John was nodding to Deirdre and shrugging at Ted. The twins were sticking their fingers in the clam dip and trying to get their grandfather to catch the crackers they were throwing at him. Luc's father was instructing the butler to make drinks at a small bar to one side of the Adam fireplace and telling the boys over his shoulder that he would be with them in a minute.

Misty cradled the baby and stared open-mouthed at a balding man sitting at the grand piano near the terrace doors. His singing was loud and flat, and his playing wasn't much better. At the same time, another plumpish man was reading him stock quotations from *The Wall Street Journal*.

"I lied when I said they were only slightly insane," Luc said into Misty's ear. He chuckled and cooed at the baby. "They're all mad."

"That's not true, Lucas Stuyvesant," his mother reproved him. "Hildebrand has a bit too much money and George tries to show him how to invest it, that's all."

"George lost a half a million dollars in oil wells last year," Luc told Misty.

"Yes, but I know for a fact that he gave an equal amount to charity," his mother supplied. She blinked rapidly at Misty. "My dear, you mustn't think my cousins gamble blindly." Her smile was indulgent as her gaze went from Misty to her son.

"They might as well just throw their money away and get it over with," Luc said dryly.

"Ah, but they have you, dear, to keep them steady." Mrs. Harrison glided away to speak to her other guests.

Misty coughed, choked, then laughed out loud. "It's so wonderful to be with your family." She gasped as the baby cooed at her. "Isn't she beautiful, Luc?"

"She's a heartbreaker," he agreed, sliding an arm around Misty's waist and leading her farther into the room.

Betsy spied them from the piano, where Hildebrand was trying to show her how to place her fingers on the keys. "Misty! Hi, Luc." She sped across the room and hugged them, then began talking nonsense to the baby. "I'm not supposed to talk baby talk to her, but she's so smart already that I don't think it will make a difference. We took care of her yesterday when Deirdre had an appointment. Marcy read her a few pages from *War and Peace*. Jenny loved it, didn't you, lovey?" The baby gurgled and waved her fists in the air. Misty and Luc laughed. His hand tightened at Misty's waist, and he kissed her on the ear.

"Oh, yuk." Betsy grimaced at them and assumed a long-suffering look as Misty's two other sisters joined them. "Are you going to drool all over each other this weekend?" Betsy asked. "I thought you were through with that stuff. You've been married for ages."

"Six weeks is not ages." Luc tapped Betsy on the nose and hugged the other girls. "You three look like bona fide collegians. Tell me what's new on the campus these days."

The three girls tugged him toward a group of chairs on one side of the room, leaving Misty alone with the baby. She chuckled as she watched her husband's family. Everyone was talking at once, all of them earnestly trying to persuade each other on whatever subject they were expounding. "It's just you and me, kid," she told the gurgling baby, who seemed to be growing restless and uncomfortable. She checked the diaper. "Ah, just as I thought. You need a change," she told Deirdre, who was still arguing with John and Ted.

"Oh, there's a diaper bag on the bed in our room. The green wing," Deirdre explained, returning immediately to her argument.

Misty shrugged. "I should be able to handle this," she said to herself. "What do you think, Jenny?"

Jenny squeezed her eyes shut and let out a howl.

No one in the room seemed to notice. Misty hurried out into the foyer and up the floating staircase to the second floor. From a past tour of the house she knew that the green wing was the biggest guest wing in the house.

After making two false turns she finally opened the correct door into Deirdre and Ted's bedroom. The diaper bag was in the center of the bed.

After placing the now squalling baby in the middle of the bed and putting pillows on either side of her, Misty stripped off the soiled diaper, disposed of it in the bathroom, and found a warm wet cloth with which to clean the baby. "Jennifer!" Misty wailed when she returned. A wet spot was spreading on the satin coverlet. "You weren't supposed to do that." The baby kicked her legs as Misty sponged her off and moved her to a dry portion of the bed, then pinned on the clean diaper. "I don't think your mother is going to appreciate my help," she told the child as she picked her up and gazed down at the dark spot in the center of the bedspread.

As Misty carried the baby down the stairs, she encountered Luc near the bottom on his way up. "I was looking for you," he said. "Where did you go?"

"Jennifer needed changing," Misty explained.

"Of course, Deirdre couldn't do that." He shot an exasperated look over his shoulder.

"I didn't mind. She's such a good baby."

Luc studied her through narrowed eyes for a minute, then came up two more steps so that their faces were even. "You look beautiful holding her," he began, then frowned. "You're pale. What is it?"

"Nothing." Misty looked away.

"You're lying to me, Mystique, and I damned well intend to find out why and what about."

"Jennifer needs her mother," she said, passing him, trying to escape his scrutinizing gaze. She hurried down the last steps and charged into the suddenly silent living room, almost tripping over the carpet in her haste.

All heads turned toward her. Hildebrand rose from the

piano. "Ah, here is the musician that Luc has married. A bit clumsy, I think." He turned to his cousin George for confirmation. "What do you say?"

"Perhaps she's a bit uncoordinated. Probably the result of poor blood lines."

"Ahhh," Hildebrand concurred, his index finger tapping the side of his nose. "That must be it."

"Shall I hold the baby while you murder them, or shall I do the deed for you?" Luc asked at her back.

"What did he say, George?" Hildebrand demanded, blinking at Luc in owlish dislike. "Lucas, must you always be so damned physical? So untidy." Hildebrand sniffed.

"If you make one more crass remark to my wife, I'll send you to the hospital, cousin. Not even my mother will protect you from that," Luc announced coolly.

Hildebrand looked for help, first from George, then from Luc's mother. "Althea, must I be subjected to this?" he demanded.

"Oh, do be quiet, Hildebrand," Luc's father said testily. He crossed the room to Misty, a broad smile on his face. "Pay no attention to him. He's a twit."

"Yes, I noticed that," Misty said clearly, the words reaching every corner of the room.

Luc's bark of laughter overrode the sighs, groans, chuckles, and exclamations of "Well, I never" that rose from the assorted company. His hand settled at Misty's waist, kneading the firm flesh.

"Perceptive little thing, isn't she?" Mr. Harrison commented to his son.

"Very," Luc agreed. "Here, darling, let me take Jennifer. She must be getting heavy."

"No," Misty said, her hands tightening on the baby. She gave her husband an apologetic glance. "I mean, I don't mind holding her for a bit longer." Unable to meet Luc's probing glance, she turned to his father. "She has your eyes," she observed, jiggling the baby in her arms and laughing out loud when she blew a bubble.

"Yes." James Harrison's shrewd gaze went from her to his son. "The Harrisons tend to have brown eyes. Perhaps you and Luc will have a brown-eyed baby."

"No, I don't think so," Misty said abruptly. "Excuse me.

I must take Jennifer to her mother." As she hurried across the room, she heard Luc and his father exchange surprised whispers, but she didn't stop.

Deirdre was still holding forth with John, while Ted was listening and grinning. Misty coughed to gain their attention.

"Ah, Mystique." Ted's grin broadened as he reached for his daughter. "How is Daddy's best girl?" Misty felt a tug on her skirt. She looked down at young James, laughing softly at his gap-toothed smile.

"Would you like to play Indians, Aunt Ma-steek? Greg and me, we gotta fort."

"Greg and I have a fort," Misty corrected absently, biting her lip as she recalled how many times her parents had corrected and criticized her. It had been so demoralizing never to hear an encouraging word from them.

"You and Greg have a fort?" James looked at her, goggle-eyed. "I didn't know that."

Misty chuckled and touched his cheek. She glanced around the room. Luc was still deeply absorbed in conversation with his father. Luc's mother and Alice were arguing about decorating. Misty's three sisters were comparing outfits. "Yes, I think I would like to see your fort," she told James. "Of course, I don't know if I can play Indians." Misty felt herself jerked forward by a strong five-year-old hand. She followed along behind, aware that Luc had lifted his head to watch her leave before refocusing his attention on his father. He was irritated with her, too, she could tell. He hated the fact that there was something she wasn't telling him. How could she explain that she wanted his child but was afraid to have it? She couldn't bury her fear that some-how she was tainted with her mother's twisted tendencies.

She shook off her dread as she followed James down a long hall and through the kitchen.

"Hi, Mabel," he called to the cook.

Misty said hello to the plump woman who was up to her elbows in flour. Her two young assistants smiled as James and Misty paraded past.

"James, why don't you call me Misty instead of Mys-tique?" she suggested. "It might be easier for you to say." They stepped from the kitchen to a damp outdoor corridor. "Isn't it too cold to play outside?"

"Yep. We're playing in the pool room. The pool is covered so it's okay to play there," James explained, leading her down a covered path to a huge bubble. "See, we could swim, but since no one is down here, the pool is covered. That way we won't fall in the water." He opened the door, letting out a blast of steamy air.

Misty welcomed the heat. Standing just inside the door, she looked around her. The olympic-sized pool was covered with a taut tarpaulin. She noted that it would be impossible for the boys to unhook the tarp from its grommets.

On the far side of the pool Greg sat on the tile floor arranging twigs as if for a fire. "He isn't going to light that, is he?" Misty's eyes widened at the thought of what a fire could do in the enormous air bubble.

"Naw. We aren't allowed to play with matches," James said matter-of-factly. "And we can't jump on the tarpaulin either, or Grandpa will skin our backsides."

"Good." Misty sighed with relief and followed the boy around the tile deck to where Greg was sitting. He ordered them to be quiet as he placed the last twig in the pile.

"There, it's done." He sighed and grinned up at Misty. "I didn't think you'd want to come, but James said you would, Aunt Ma-steek."

"We're supposed to call her Aunt Misty now," James announced importantly.

"Oh." Greg reached behind him and pulled a pheasant feather from a bag. He handed it to her. "Here. We found these on our farm. You wear it with this." He searched in the bag again and pulled out a garter, which he also handed to her.

Misty lifted an eyebrow at the blue satin garter with pink rosebuds and ruffles. "This is a bride's garter." She paused at the sight of their guarded expressions.

Greg shrugged. "It's ugly, I know, but it was all I could find in Mom's drawer. Grandma gave us these round ones. Aren't they neat?" He held up two more garters. "She said her mother used to roll her stockings in them." He looked puzzled for a moment, then shrugged. "I can't figure it out, but in the old days they did weird things."

"Right." Misty was glad now that she and Luc hadn't changed out of their travel clothes. She had no trouble sitting with the boys around their "fire." She slipped the garter over her head, inserted the feather, and passed the peace pipe, an intricately carved meerschaum. She was afraid it belonged to their father or grandfather.

"Ugh," Misty answered when Greg gestured that they stand and dance around the fire. "Whooo, whooo, whooo . . ." Misty chanted as she danced with half-closed eyes.

"Good God, she's a primitive." Hildebrand's voice carried clearly across the room. Misty gasped and whirled around. The sight that met her eyes made her want to sink through the floor. Luc's whole family was clustered just inside the door, watching her with astonished expressions.

CHAPTER EIGHT

MISTY PAUSED WITH one foot in midair, her palm inches from her open mouth, her eyes going as if in slow motion from one member of the family to the next. She froze when she saw Luc, his arms folded across his chest, standing next to his mother. "How, paleface," she said, turning her palm outward in a greeting.

"How," Luc murmured, raising one hand in imitation of hers.

"Me Red Eagle," Greg said, thumping his chest.

"Me Running Deer," James said with a fierce scowl.

"Me Purple Chicken," Misty finished lamely.

"Me Great Hunter coming to get Purple Chicken," Luc announced in deep tones, setting off peals of laughter among the family.

George and Hildebrand tutted and muttered. "No one need know she's related to us," said Hildebrand. "We could say she's a bit soft in her upper works," said George.

"Damnation, is that my meerschaum pipe?" Ted exclaimed.

"Is that my wedding garter around your head, Mystique?" Deirdre asked shrilly.

"What do you mean, yours?" Alice swelled with anger. "I let you borrow it. It's mine."

Misty turned questioning eyes to the boys. They shrugged sheepishly. "Fine braves you are," she mumbled as she pulled the offending garter and feather from her head. "Now it's every man for himself, I suppose."

"Just don't say too much," Greg whispered from the side of his mouth as the grownups came toward them from both sides of the pool. "Uncle Luc and Dad will take care of it."

"Yeah. Act like it never happened, Purple Chicken," James advised.

"Thanks, you two," Misty muttered as Luc ambled toward her, a gleam in his eye, his mother at his side.

"Not that I don't think you look absolutely smashing with the feather, dear," said Althea. "I do. You have marvelous clothes sense, but I'm not sure how our other guests will react. Of course, when all is said and done, who really cares what others think?" She smiled reassuringly at Misty. "I think you're perfect for Lucas." She kissed Misty's cheek and glanced over at the boys. "You've made good use of those garters. What smart lads you are!" Her grandsons beamed.

"They're brilliant," Luc's father insisted, skillfully inserting himself between the boys and their irate mother and aunt. "Come along with me, now. Mabel has a nice drink for you." He put his hands on their shoulders. As they walked away, Misty thought she heard him add conspiratorially, "Now, let's get out of here." But she wasn't sure.

"After dinner I'll have Hawes remove the cover and take you swimming," called their grandmother.

"This isn't the end of it," Deirdre warned her sons, glaring when her husband chuckled.

"I do believe they're almost as bad as our sons were," Alice said thoughtfully.

"Never," John denied, ushering his wife back to the main house. As the others departed, one by one, Misty and Luc were left alone.

"Great Hunter think Purple Chicken very sexy." Luc

leaned toward her and ran a hand over her suede-covered thigh.

"It will cost you much wampum to flirt with Purple Chicken," she informed him.

"Oh? How much?" Luc bit her earlobe and blew in her ear, sending tingles down to her toes.

"The scalps of those two braves who left me holding the bag." With effort Misty suppressed a smile.

"Old Indian maxim say: Never trust any of the Harrison tribe."

"Heap good advice." Misty closed her eyes as Luc's mouth touched hers. The kiss deepened, and her body sagged against him. His arms took her full weight as they swayed in sensual enjoyment.

"Shall I take off the tarpaulin so we can swim?" he suggested.

"Could we?"

"Uh-huh. I'll lock the door when we leave and tell Hawes what we've done. He won't let the boys in here alone."

"But we need suits."

"Hell, no." Luc held her back from him for a moment, his eyes serious. "You don't trust me fully yet, Mrs. Harrison, but you will."

"Luc," Misty began, but he turned away from her and strode along the deck to a cabana, returning a moment later with what appeared to be a large wrench. He knelt down at the far end of the pool and twisted off several grommets with the tool. After releasing that end of the tarpaulin, he folded it over, then went from side to side, loosening the rest of the grommets. Misty tried to help him fold the tarpaulin, but she found the sagging canvas too heavy. Instead, he used a hand crank to lift it off the pool.

"There. We'll leave it at one end like that," said Luc. "Hawes and a couple of the other men can put it away." He rose to his feet and stared across at her. "Come along, Mrs. Harrison. We'll undress in the cabana."

"Luc, what if someone comes?"

"Don't worry. I'll lock the door and put a sign on the outside." He held up an oblong cardboard that said in big letters: DO NOT DISTURB—SWIMMING NUDE.

Misty gasped. "Where did you get that?"

"John had it made for Mother and Dad as a joke, but they've actually used it a few times." He chuckled.

"And you?" Misty asked sharply.

Luc's eyes glinted. "I've swum nude with women a few times."

"More than a few, I'll bet," Misty said tartly.

"Darling, how you talk." He came around to lead her to the cabana.

She struggled to control her anger and jealousy at the thought of Luc swimming nude with other women. But the emotions burned in her, like raging flames. When she tried to close the cabana door against Luc, he pushed it open. "No way. We undress together."

Misty turned her back to him as she undressed, too upset to speak. The man had the power to make her temper go wild for no sensible reason! It angered and befuddled her to think that she was so easily riled by him.

"Ummm, so nice. You have the most gorgeous skin of any woman I've ever known." Luc's hand feathered over her backside.

"Spare me the detailed catalog of the women you've known," she snapped.

"Am I getting to you, darling? I hope so." He hung her vest and blouse next to his trousers.

She whirled around to retort, clad just in her briefs, but the sight of his naked body brought her up short. As she scanned his strong, muscular form, his skin taut and glistening, throbbing desire came alive in her. He took hold of her upper arms. "I hope I'm getting to you because you get to me. I'm frustrated. My wife is keeping something from me. Don't try to deny it."

"I'm not," she mumbled.

"And it makes me furious. So I dig away at you, trying to make you irritated enough to tell me what's buried under that red-gold hair of yours." Luc stared grimly down at her.

"Luc, I . . . I have something to sort out."

"Damn you, Mystique, why won't you tell me?"

"Are we going to swim?" she asked, desperate to change the subject.

He ground his teeth in frustration, then reached out and

slipped the silky briefs from her body. "Now we are."

Relief flooded through her as he took her hand. She needed him so much . . . But she couldn't tell him about how she felt about giving birth.

Luc lifted her in his arms. "Don't." Misty laughed, anticipating what he meant to do.

"It's you and me, love, all the way." Without further preamble he jumped into the deep end of the pool, taking her down with him into the chlorinated depths.

Misty didn't panic at the sudden loss of oxygen. She relaxed completely as Luc turned her to face him. His mouth came over hers, and he breathed his own life-sustaining air into her as they reversed direction and rose slowly to the surface.

Misty lifted her head above water with oxygen to spare, but she saw at once that Luc was gasping for breath. Humility coursed through her. Luc had given her the very air from his lungs, as well as shown the caring and sharing she had found as a married woman. He had done all that for her, although she had never expected it from him.

She paddled closer. He treaded water, watching her warily. He expected her to dunk him, she realized as he took a deep breath. "Darling," she murmured, tracing her fingers over his open mouth, his slowly moving feet keeping her easily afloat. Her mouth followed her fingers, and her hands crept upward into his hair. It struck her like a blow that there was no need for her to *tell* Luc she loved him. She need only love him at every opportunity. The realization left her feeling as light as air. For a moment she forgot to kick her legs and began to sink.

Luc's hands were immediately at her waist, hoisting her up again before she knew it. "What are you thinking, love?" he asked hoarsely. "Damn you. All you have to do is touch me, and I start to crumble like a cracker."

"My mind's blank," she told him serenely, her eyes half closed as she moved her body against his, her breasts tingling at the touch of his slick body. The softened hair on his chest rubbing against her skin created a sensual massage.

Luc clenched his hands on her hips. She was driving him wild. "Who would ever think that making love standing up in fifteen feet of water could be so delightful?" he said with a growl, manacling her to his hard thighs.

"I thought cold water was supposed to make that impossible." Misty rubbed her thigh in a gentle rhythm against his aroused body.

"With you, cold water is only another inducement, darling," Luc crooned, caressing her with skillful fingers, making her cry out with need for him.

She slid her arms around his neck and twined her legs around his waist. "I surrender," she whispered in his ear.

"Damn you, Mystique. Darling..." Luc sank with his burden under the water, then shot to the surface. He lifted her to the tile deck and vaulted up beside her. But instead of letting her rise, he pressed her down on the tiles and reached for a stack of fluffy towels.

"Your mother will think you're very extravagant using all those towels," she murmured as he spread them out, then lifted her onto their softness.

"I don't want your delicate flesh to get bruised, darling." Their wet bodies slid together with mounting need, awakening a thousand nerve endings. Misty was overwhelmed with throbbing, pulsating sensations.

"I'm here, Mystique." Luc kissed her ankle and nibbled on her Achilles tendon, setting off a series of exquisite shocks.

"My goodness," she said, gasping. "Whoever would have guessed that a leg could be so sensitive?" Her head rolled back and forth on the soft towels.

"I've had crazy sensations since the first time I saw your legs, darling," Luc muttered, his tongue searching for and finding her most intimate source of feeling.

"I...I..." Misty forgot what she was going to say as her body lifted and arched in an ecstatic consummation. Luc joined with her, and together they shot through the roof of the world, wrapped together in the ultimate joy of giving to each other.

His chest was still heaving when he pulled her on top of him and pressed tiny kisses on her face. "You're my angel."

"I want to be," she told him, aware that she had just given over a bit more of her life to him, that each time they made love he possessed more of her. It frightened her to give so much of herself, but she couldn't help it. She knew that she was far and away deeper into Luc's life than she had ever approached with Richard and Leonard.

"Misty, don't withdraw from me into that private corner of your mind where I can't go. I hate it when you do that," Luc grumbled. "I want to dynamite my way into your most intimate thoughts."

"Violent man," Misty chided.

A banging on the outside door startled both of them. "Hey, you two," called Ted. "The ponies are in the corral, and it's time to eat, and Hawes would like to get in there, and—"

"All right, Ted, we hear you," Luc interrupted, rising and pulling Misty to her feet, cuddling her to his body. "Tell Hawes not to worry. I took off the tarp. He can put it away. We'll be there in a minute."

"Right. I brought down the clothes that were laid out on your bed. I'll put them on the bench out here. Hurry it up. You wouldn't want your clothes to freeze." Ted chuckled. his voice fading as he returned to the house.

Misty looked anxiously up at Luc. "They'll know what we've been doing."

He nodded, unperturbed. "I should hope so. We've only been married a short time. My sisters and parents can't be so dense that they don't remember what it's like." He kissed her nose. "Darling, stop looking so worried." He strode over to the outer door and cursed the blast of cold air that swept in as he retrieved their clothes. "Hurry up," he called. "I want to take a warm shower." Grinning, he rushed her into the dressing room, holding up her outfit. "See? Your silk dress will be nice and fresh from the steam."

"How can you be so unconcerned!" Misty demanded, her hands clenching into fists. "We'll have to walk into that living room."

Luc shot out his wrist to look at his watch and shook his head. "I shouldn't think so. They'll be sitting down to dinner about now. We'll walk into the dining room."

"That's worse," Misty cried, sagging against him as he led her into the shower and helped her wash the chlorine from her hair and body.

"There's a hair dryer, darling, and an infrared lamp." He showed her where everything was. "Don't worry."

In her embarrassment she fumbled more than once, slowing her progress. Finally Luc fastened her dress for her. "Ummm, I love you in silk. So sexy . . ."

"Luc, we're late." Misty slapped his hand away from her thigh and glared at him when he laughed. In spite of herself she could feel her own mouth lifting in amusement. "You're awful."

"So sue me. I'm a bridegroom," he drawled, kissing the corner of her mouth, which she had just put lipstick on.

"Luc, stop," she wailed as he scooped her into his arms again and gave her a deep kiss. "Ohhh . . ." she moaned, "I should hit you."

"Umm, lovely. Hit me." He nibbled on her neck.

She pushed against his chest with both hands. "We have to go—right this minute." Scrambling past him, she raced out of the dressing room to the outer door.

"I think there's a law against abusing husbands," he crooned in her ear as he followed her at a trot along the path to the back door of the house.

Misty inhaled the warm, yeasty smell of the kitchen just as Mabel came through the swinging door leading to the dining room.

"Aha!" she declared, facing them, arms akimbo. "Love may be a fine thing, but the soup's getting cold." Misty blushed, and Luc chuckled.

"Sorry, Mabel, my darling." Luc placed a smacking kiss on her plump cheek just before swinging wide the double doors to the dining room and propelling Misty through them into the crowded room. Murmured conversation and the clinking of china and silver greeted them.

"There they are," young James caroled. "We get to stay for the soup, Aunt Misty, and then we're going to the pool. Did you have a nice swim?"

All eyes turned to Misty as everyone awaited her answer. "Ummm, great," Luc drawled. He let out a burst of laughter, bringing every eye to him. The adults shot quick glances at the boys as they, too, joined in the laughter.

"If I'd known you like swimming that much, Aunt Misty, I would have had gone with you," Greg interjected.

The adults' laughter grew louder as Luc led Misty to her seat. She was burning with embarrassment, blushing to the roots of her hair. "Thank you, dears," she mumbled to the boys, earning beaming smiles in return.

Misty lifted a soup spoon to her mouth, noticed that everyone was quiet, and looked up to find every eye on her. She swallowed the soup, hoping it wouldn't go down the wrong way and returned the spoon to the plate.

"You don't slurp," Greg observed from across the table. "That's good. Now you won't have to leave the table."

"And isn't that a blessing?" Luc whispered in her ear.

"Why does Uncle Luc keep biting your ear, Aunt Misty?" James asked.

Laughter rose again, then was masked behind coughs and throat clearings.

"Because, James," Luc answered for her, "Uncle Luc loves Purple Chicken."

Misty's heart seemed to soar away on a cloud of happiness. Everyone around her was laughing. Even she was laughing. But deep inside she knew it was a matter of deepest importance to have heard Luc say those words.

"Love agrees with you, Mystique, my dear." Her father-in-law leaned forward in his chair as Hawes led the twins away from the table to go for their swim. "You're positively glowing."

"She's beautiful," Luc said simply, rubbing his lips against her temple in a sensual massage.

She stared at him. "Stop it," she whispered, flushing.

"Don't try to control Luc, Mystique," Alice advised her. "He was always unruly as a boy."

"He was a knothead," Deirdre announced irreverently.

"Now, girls," Mrs. Harrison said placatingly.

Misty was stunned by the feeling of outrage that took hold of her at Luc's sisters' teasing. They were joking, she knew. Families often talked like that among themselves. But an irrational part of her resented the remarks, because she remembered how her parents had criticized her.

"Misty doesn't like you saying that," said Celia.

Betsy giggled. "I'll say. I remember her looking that way sometimes when we were small."

"Yes, I remember when Roddy Gordon pulled the cat's tail," said Marcy. "Misty socked him in the eye and brought the cat home, but Mother wouldn't let us keep it. Aunt

Lizabeth and Uncle Charlie took it. They had it for twelve years." Marcy's voice faded as the sisters regarded one another.

"That's my girl," Luc said, kissing Misty's cheek. "Defender of the weak and homeless."

Chuckles rose from around the table. As Misty gazed at each of the family members, her anger faded, she lost her self-consciousness, and the warmth of acceptance enveloped her.

After dinner everyone went into the living room for coffee, each one settling into a favorite chair. Mrs. Harrison sat down in front of a massive coffee service on a marble-top table.

"I suppose Mystique will play for us," Hildebrand said with a long-suffering expression.

"Only if you pay her," Luc snapped. "My wife is a professional musician, not a bumbling amateur like you."

"Really, Althea! Can't you control your son?" Hildebrand sniffed with disdain.

Mrs. Harrison seemed to consider his comment for a moment. "No, I don't think I can. Luc has always been strong-minded." She smiled at Misty. "Dearest Mystique, you don't have to play, but I must say I enjoyed listening to you that evening in the Edwardian Room when Luc took us to hear you. You have such a light touch."

Misty rose, smiling at her mother-in-law. "Of course I'll play for you, if you like."

"Please." Mrs. Harrison beamed, ignoring Luc's irritated gaze.

Misty went to the piano, flexing her fingers and rubbing her wrists. She raised her hands over the keys, and Rachmaninoff flowed forth before she had consciously made the decision to play his music. The driving rhythms and haunting melody seemed a perfect expression of her inner turmoil. As she swung one of his rhapsodies, she lost herself completely in the music.

When she paused, suddenly worried that Luc's family might have preferred to hear something lighter, there came a burst of applause. She looked up, surprised. A sigh of relief escaped her as Luc approached the piano.

He leaned toward her and whispered in her ear, "I feel

so proud of you. You never fail to surprise me, darling. You play magnificently." He kissed her hand. "Would you play 'Something Was Missing' just as you played it for me the other night?"

Misty nodded happily. So, he *had* known she'd been playing the song just for him that evening in the Edwardian Room. "Will you stand there"—she pointed in front of the piano—"where I can see you?" Luc nodded and positioned himself in the curve of the grand piano, his relaxed stance belied by the kinetic energy flashing in his eyes.

Misty sang the lovely lyrics straight from the heart to him.

As the last notes died away, applause once more filled the room. "Bravo, darling, bravo," Luc murmured to her alone.

"Oh, Luc," she began, tears stinging her eyes.

"Gee, Misty, you're good," Betsy said. "I'd forgotten how well you played."

"My dear . . ." Tears shone in Althea's eyes, too, as she came forward with her hands outstretched. "How beautiful you are."

Misty basked in the sunshine of their attentiveness. Her glance slid to her sisters, who were assuring Alice that there was no need to buy a grand piano; they had never studied music.

"But I always wanted to," Betsy finished wistfully.

"Ha!" Alice declared, a zealot's light in her eyes. "We shall find you a top-notch teacher on Monday."

"Lord," Luc muttered, holding Misty to his side, his eyes on John. "How many Steinways will you have to buy, do you think?"

"I'm not sure," John mumbled, a fascinated eye on his wife as she told Misty's sisters how well rounded they would be once they had studied both music and watercolors.

"It's very good for the spirit to paint," she finished.

"But I can't draw a straight line," Betsy said faintly.

"Don't worry." Alice patted her arm. "I'm sure John can find a teacher who would rather work with circles and curves than lines."

"Can you do that, John?" Luc queried his brother-in-law, tongue in cheek.

"You're a rat," he said mildly.

"Luc, rescue him," Misty pleaded. "Don't let Alice get all those teachers for my sisters."

Luc's eyes were like brown lasers searing her with sudden desire. "Let's go up to our room . . . Then I'll talk to Alice." His husky words filled her with longing, but she was acutely conscious of the people around them.

"Luc, please. Your father is looking at us."

Luc shrugged. "I don't care who's looking. Tomorrow when all those people arrive we won't have any time alone."

She couldn't help but chuckle at his woeful expression, which became thunderous when she laughed. "It's not funny," he declared.

She ran a fingernail down his nose. *"You're* funny."

"Take me to bed," he drawled, bending over her, his hands sliding to her waist.

"Not now," she said, chuckling. "We were in bed just a while ago."

"We weren't in bed. We made love on the pool deck. Now I want to make love in our bed. Let's go home."

"We can't!" The blood grew hot in her veins as Luc continued to look down at her with undisguised desire.

"Why?" He rubbed his mouth on hers. "Your heart is beating as fast as mine." He pressed the palm of his hand to her chest, his fingers splayed on the soft flesh.

"Luc," she whispered hoarsely as her pulse skyrocketed. "Maybe we could . . ."

They were turning to leave the room when Hildebrand come up to them. "Well, Mystique, you really surprised me," he said loftily. "Your technique isn't half bad." He paused momentarily as he noticed Luc's furious expression. "Ah, you're all red, cousin. You look—" he laughed "—as if you want to kill someone." Hildebrand's mouth slackened as Luc lifted his hand from Misty's waist and flexed it into a fist. "Pardon me. I have to see someone." With a shudder Hildebrand walked stiffly away.

"Luc . . ." Misty rested her head on his chest. "You shouldn't intimidate him like that. He thinks you're serious about hitting him."

"I am," Luc said, hugging her when she laughed. "Umm, I love the feel of your breasts pressed tight to me."

"Stop!" She was laughing out loud now, attracting the attention of several people nearby.

"Let's take a walk," he suggested.

"We'll have to get our coats."

"No. We'll walk through the house. This place is huge. I'll show you some of the galleries that are closed off most of the time."

Misty's skin tingled in delight as Luc took her hand and they walked up the wide staircase. They passed through the corridor to their room and went down another narrower hallway that lay beyond the master suite occupied by Luc's parents. At the end, double oak doors led to a small foyer. "This is called the turquoise wing," Luc explained, "but I suspect the only turquoise thing here is the mold." He grinned at her and reached up to take from the lintel a key which he inserted in the lock. "Just as I thought—a little musty."

"It's not too bad, Luc." Misty's whispered words echoed in the unused room. Her eyes settled on a painting of a woman working at a loom. "That reminds me." She nodded at the painting. "Did I ever tell you how grateful I am that you granted Morey a loan?"

"Yes, you did. Now be quiet so I can kiss you." Luc pulled her into his arms, and his mouth came down on hers.

"But—" Misty gasped and pulled slightly away from him. "I don't think you realize what you did for him. It was so kind."

"I was kind because he was your friend. Don't make it out to be more than it was. I would have done anything to get in your good graces."

Misty's heart flipped over. How she loved to hear him say things like that! "It was still very kind of you," she insisted, "and he won't fail you, Luc. He's an excellent designer."

"I agree. I've seen some of his designs—the clothes you wear for work." He frowned. "Not that I like to see you so bare . . ."

"Luc!" She was chuckling as she took his head between her hands. "You're very sweet."

Powerful silence filled the room as they stared intently into each other's eyes, facing each other like living, breathing statues frozen forever in a moment of perfect love.

Gently Luc placed his hands over hers on his face. "Mystique." The whispered word echoed in the empty room. "I want us to have a baby."

CHAPTER NINE

ALL DURING THE rest of their stay Misty was aware of Luc's hurt and frustration with her. She'd stiffened in his arms at his mention of children, and, despite his frequent efforts to get her to reveal what was troubling her, she was still unable to share her fears about becoming a mother.

When they returned home Sunday evening, she told him, "Luc, I'm not hungry. I'm going straight to bed."

"I want to talk to you."

"Please, not now. In the morning." Misty felt his anger radiating like heat waves on her back as she turned and left the kitchen. Wearily she climbed the stairs to their bedroom.

Much to her surprise, she fell asleep immediately after a quick shower. When she awoke the next morning Luc was already gone, and though his blankets were mussed she had no recollection of him even having come to bed. She had a splitting headache, one so severe that she became sick to her stomach. She was holding a cold cloth to her forehead when the phone rang.

"Mrs. Harrison, this is Dr. Wagner's office. You said to call you if there was a cancellation."

"Yes?"

"We have an opening at two o'clock today, if you'd like to take it."

"Yes, I'll be there." Misty hung up the phone and sat back in bed. Did she have the flu? She sighed, determined to keep the appointment with her gynecologist no matter how ill she felt.

By noon she was feeling somewhat better, much to her relief. She took a vitamin pill, but she didn't eat anything. Her stomach hadn't completely settled down.

At one o'clock she left the house, on impulse taking the bus to Henri Bendel, something Luc had been urging her to do since the beginning of their marriage.

As she walked into the quietly elegant establishment, she felt relaxed. She found some gloves in the softest white kid that she could use for evening wear and purchased several handkerchiefs with which to wipe her hands between musical arrangements at work.

By the time she left the store she was running late and had to take a taxi to the doctor's office, instead of waiting for the bus as she had planned.

She didn't have to wait long to see Dr. Wagner, and the examination was thorough but not uncomfortable. Afterward she got dressed, ran a comb through her hair, and met the doctor back in her office.

"I hope you'll be able to suggest another method of birth control," Misty began. "As you know, I was on the pill, but—" She stopped short in response to the quizzical look the doctor was giving her. "What's wrong, Dr. Wagner?"

The doctor closed Misty's folder and placed her elbows on top, her chin in her hands. "Misty," she said gently, "you're several weeks pregnant. Didn't you know?"

Misty's stomach seemed to sink to her feet. She stared at the doctor in stunned disbelief as a horrible sense of unreality swept over her. "I was tired," she said through stiff lips, "but I thought I might have the flu. I've never had regular periods." She let out a strangled sob. "I can't have this baby."

Dr. Wagner sat back in her chair and regarded Misty with concern. "You're very healthy, Misty, and I foresee no problem with the pregnancy, but if you insist on an abortion, I can suggest a colleague."

"Abortion? No, I don't want that. I'll give the baby up for adoption."

"You're married, Misty. Why would you want to do that?" Dr. Wagner asked with evident confusion.

"I'm married, that's true," Misty said dully.

"Doesn't your husband want children?"

"He loves them," Misty choked out, then bit her lip and fell silent. She stared sightlessly down at her hands.

"Misty," Dr. Wagner said, "something is deeply troubling you. Please tell me what it is so that I can try to help."

Misty studied the other woman's kind, concerned face, and suddenly knew she wanted to tell her everything. Words began to pour out of her in an unstoppable flood. She began at the very beginning, by describing how her essentially happy childhood had led to a traumatic adolescence. She explained how her parents had constantly corrected and criticized her and finally condemned her as an unworthy daughter. She went on to describe how her life had improved under her aunt and uncle's loving care, but how the vestiges of her low self-esteem had allowed her to get involved with Richard and Leonard, two men who used rather than loved her. Finally she told how Luc had entered her life and made her recovery complete. Except that she knew she must never have a child and risk becoming a destructive and hate-filled mother like her own.

When Misty finished, Dr. Wagner shook her head. "Misty, I grant you that there is sound evidence to support your belief that many emotionally abused children become abusive parents. But you've already faced and dealt with your problem. That makes all the difference in the world."

"But what if I...I..." To Misty's horror, tears filled her eyes and spilled onto her cheeks.

Dr. Wagner came around the desk, pressed a tissue into Misty's fingers, and laid a comforting hand on her shoulder. "Talk to your husband, my dear. Then come back to me, and we'll all three talk together. I sense that you do want this baby."

"Yes," she admitted with wrenching pain. She drew in several deep, steadying breaths, struggling to regain emotional control.

"Don't deny motherhood because you fear yourself," Dr. Wagner added. "Go back to your therapist. I'm sure he will tell you the same thing."

"Yes, yes, I'll make an appointment to see him." Misty wiped her eyes, a whisper of hope uncurling deep inside her.

Once outside, Misty began walking home, too deep in thought to even think of taking a bus or a cab. By the time she walked in the front door, she was tired and cold.

The sounds of someone in the kitchen surprised her. Mrs. Wheaton should have gone home hours ago. "Mrs. Wheaton, I'm home," she called. "I sure would love a cup of tea." She pushed open the door and stopped in her tracks. "Luc! What are you doing home so early?"

"Where the hell have you been?" he demanded. "More to the point, why didn't you take your car? Did you go on the subway? Damn it, Mystique, don't you know how dangerous that can be?"

Misty remained stunned into speechlessness as Luc rattled off question after question. When he received no answers from her, he strode forward and pulled her into his arms. She sighed with delight and weariness as his muscular heat enclosed her. "Ummm, you're so toasty warm," she murmured.

"Damn you, Mystique. I don't want you riding around Manhattan on a bus or subway." He leaned back to look at her. "Now, where were you?" He spotted the bag crushed between them. "Bendel's! So that's where you were. But why didn't you drive?"

"Sometimes I forget that I can take a cab or drive a car whenever I choose," she answered truthfully.

"Well, try to remember from now on, okay? I don't like coming home and not finding you here. I called Mrs. Wheaton to tell her to defrost some fish for us." He frowned. "That's why I came home early, so we could fix lemon sole together."

"Wonderful. Just let me take a shower and change first."

"I'll shower with you."

"No. We'll never get around to eating."

"Yes, we will. At midnight."

Misty shook her head and backed out into the hall. "No way. I'm hungry." She was laughing as she ran up the stairs, finally able to push her problem to the back of her mind.

She'd finished her shower and was humming to herself as, clad only in a silky bra and briefs, she searched through her closet for something to wear.

"I knew I'd find you like this." Luc's silky voice sent shivers up her spine and wave after wave of sensual shocks through her.

"It seems to me," Misty said sternly, straightening slowly but not turning around, "that you're always finding me in my underthings."

"Right," Luc said huskily, walking up behind her. "I was trying to think up an excuse for barging in on you like this, but"—he leaned down and kissed the nape of her neck—"I knew you'd see right through every one of them."

"Right," she agreed dryly, closing her eyes and letting herself relax against him.

"Ahh, good," he whispered, satisfaction in his voice as his hands began an intimate exploration of her rib cage. "You're gaining weight," he murmured. "That's good."

Misty reeled back in shock. Was it possible that he'd already noticed a slight difference in her shape? She closed her eyes, trying to resummon her quickly vanishing emotional equilibrium.

"Luc . . ." She lifted her hands from where they lay on top of his around her waist. "Let me go, please." The words were barely audible.

Immediately his hands fell from her, and he stepped back. "Are you going to tell me what's wrong?" He sounded angry.

Misty met his steady gaze. "Let me get my dressing gown first."

"I'll get it," he snapped, striding over to the bed where she had thrown the robe after emerging from the bathroom. He faced her with the dressing gown in his hands. "Turn around. I have a feeling I'm not going to like this."

She put her arms into the gown and belted it at the waist, then walked to the elegant chaise longue and stood behind it, facing him. "Luc, I went to the doctor today . . . to get a prescription for birth control pills."

"Mystique, if you don't want children right away, we can discuss it."

"Luc, listen. Dr. Wagner examined me. It was a very thorough examination." She took a deep breath. "The fact is, I'm pregnant."

His mouth dropped open. A smile lifted the corners and glinted in his eyes. "Darling..."

"Luc," Misty said on a sob, biting her lip, "I...I'm not going to keep the baby."

"You want an abortion?" he barked furiously, his hands clenching at his sides.

"No...no, I couldn't do that to our child. I intend to carry it full term, then release it for adoption." She watched miserably for his reaction, pleading silently for him to understand.

"And what if I don't want my child to be raised by strangers?"

She forced herself to say the words. "If you insist on keeping the child, I'll leave you."

"I see," he said with a calmness belied by his tense stance. "I thought you loved children. Were you only pretending to enjoy playing with Greg and James? Did you actually feel loathing when you cooed at Jennifer?"

"No, of course not," she shot back, stung that he should think such things. "I love them."

"What about Mark and Mary?" he demanded as though she hadn't spoken. "Did you only pretend to be fond of them? And what did you feel for Janie Patterson, my sister Vel's girl, whom you met at Christmas? Was it all a charade when you took them all skating?"

"No, no, no!" Misty denied, shaking her head and holding out a hand to make him stop. "Can't you see?" she screamed. "I can't take a chance that I might become like my mother!"

Luc's face twisted with anger. "Do you have so little faith in yourself that you'd rather give our child away than trust your own strength?" he demanded incredulously.

Misty felt as though he'd slapped her face. "But don't you see?" she wailed. "I can't take the risk."

"Damn you for being a coward, Mystique," he said

harshly, conflicting emotions of anger and love warring in his face.

"Yes, yes, I am a coward!" she cried.

He didn't reply. They stood facing each other like hostile opponents, their breathing harsh in the stillness.

"Get dressed. We have to fix dinner," Luc said with calm authority.

"I'm not hungry."

"You're eating for the baby," he reminded her. "And stop looking at me as though you think I'm going to strike you."

"I don't think that," Misty whispered, shivering. No, she knew he wouldn't ever hit her, but his anger was almost as frightening as physical violence.

He regarded her through narrowed eyes. "Dammit, do you think I'm going to attack you the way your father did? Berate you? Unfairly accuse you? Cut you down with words?" He inhaled a furious breath and exhaled it shakily. He studied her for long minutes. "I freely admit I'm angry with you, but that does not mean I don't understand how you feel. I don't agree with you, that's all. And I intend to spend the next eight months or so proving that you can trust me and yourself." His voice softened. "You *can* trust me, Mystique. Do you hear me?"

"I think they hear you on Long Island," she said dryly.

"As long as *you* hear me," he replied with faint amusement. "Now, are you going to get dressed or shall I do it for you?" His eyes went to her middle. "You *are* getting bigger," he said with quiet satisfaction. "Are you well? There aren't any complications, are there?"

"No problems. I have to take vitamins and eat whole cereals." She shrugged. "You know, the usual stuff for a pregnant woman."

Luc patted his shirt pocket as though looking for something. "No, I don't know, but I'll learn. Do you have paper and pencil? I want to get this down." He went to her desk, found some paper, and began writing rapidly. "Didn't you get any more details? Never mind, I'll call the doctor in the morning."

"Luc..." Misty reached into her closet for a pair of velvet jeans in a soft rose color and a matching silk blouse.

"I made an appointment with Dr. Mellon, the therapist I used to go to."

"When you first began taking charge of your life. Now you want to see him, but you don't trust your instincts."

"I do for myself, Luc," she tried to explain, "but I can't take any chances with our child. I just can't."

"Fine. Neither can I. I'll go with you to see Dr. Mellon. I have a few latent eccentricities he can begin to deal with. No, I am not laughing at you," he assured her. "I'm as serious as you are. I fully intend to be a very good parent . . . and a better husband." He held out his hand to her. "If talking to a therapist will help me in any way, then I'll work with him." Luc dropped his hand when she made no move to take it.

"I believe you, Luc," she said.

He let out a deep breath. "Well, that's a start." She pulled on soft rose-colored ankle boots, then straightened. "You look very beautiful in that color," he said. "Renoir would have loved to paint you. Your hair is red-gold. Your eyes are far more luminous than your emerald ring." He gave her a half smile. "I think I should be your PR man as well as your husband."

"Yes," Misty agreed softly, grateful that his anger had faded. She wanted back the teasing, loving Luc who was hers alone.

He reached out to pull her toward him. "I tossed a coin to see who'll make the salad. You lost." Together they headed downstairs.

"Was it a two-headed coin?"

"Why, wife, how you talk!" he drawled, running the flat of his hand down over her backside. "Ummm, you do have everything in the proper place, don't you?"

Misty laughed, leaning against him and daring to hope that, just maybe, they would find a solution to her problem, that just maybe Luc was right and she wouldn't have to give up her baby. She erased her thoughts of the pain and concentrated on the man walking down the staircase beside her, their bodies bumping gently at every step.

In the kitchen Luc rinsed the fish in cold water, soaked it in fresh lemon juice, and let it drain. Misty paused in tearing fresh spinach leaves for a salad and watched him, delighted by his off-key whistling.

"Stop goofing off," he chided her with a grin, wiping his hands on a towel he had thrown over one shoulder. "I'm doing all the work."

"Poor baby," Misty cooed.

He breathed in sharply. "When you pout like that, my blood pressure goes up thirty points. Love, your face is getting red. How far does your blush go?" Chuckling, he reached for the belt at her waist and brought her close, her hands still full of spinach leaves. "All the way down there," he whispered, lifting the neck of her silk blouse so that he could look down.

"You should be arrested," Misty declared, laughing. "You're a devil."

"Uh-uh, just a husband."

"Do you think all husbands are so interested in their wives?"

"They would be if they were married to you. But no one except me is ever going to have that privilege. You're mine for the next ninety years. After that you're on your own." Luc kissed her open mouth.

"By the same token, you're mine for the next ninety years."

"By George, I think she's got it. Now finish that salad. I have to make a few phone calls." He kissed her temple and left the room.

"Bossy." Misty sighed, feeling free from worry for the first time all day. "Don't get too comfortable," she muttered to herself. But her admonition didn't dispel the happiness that filled her. She was here with Luc. They were together!

"Daydreaming?" Luc asked from the doorway. She looked up to see him lounging against the frame.

"Never." Forcing herself not to smile, she pretended to glare at him.

"Looked like it to me." He ambled over toward her and leaned down to kiss her. "I'll put the coffee on."

"You usually do that after we've eaten."

"Tonight we might be having guests before we're finished."

"Oh? You didn't mention that anyone would be stopping by." Misty popped a spinach leaf into her mouth.

"That was before I informed my mother that she's to have another grandchild in September." Luc licked the corner of her mouth. "Piece of spinach there," he explained.

"Ah, Luc, do you think you should—"

"Yes, I do think I should inform the family. In fact, I'm thinking of putting an announcement in *The New York Times*."

"Luc!" Misty laughed as he left her to check the saffron rice and the sole, which was turning golden brown under the broiler.

They took their food into the dining room and sat at right angles to each other. Misty tasted the fish. "Ummm, good." She smacked her lips. "I've been so hungry, lately."

Luc grinned at her. "Expectant mamas have big appetites, but I intend to see that you go on a very special diet. You and our child will have the best health care."

Misty stared in awe at the gleam of determination in his eyes. "Dr. Wagner didn't say I needed a special diet," she began, falling silent as Luc glowered at her.

"What does she know?"

"She's the doctor," Misty pointed out softly.

"I'll talk to her in the morning."

Misty argued with him, but nothing she said shook him from his stand. They were still discussing the subject as they cleared the table and did the dishes. As they finished, the doorbell rang.

"That must be my mother and father," Luc said, smiling.

Misty turned to him in astonishment. "You let them drive all the way in here from Long Island tonight?" she accused.

He shrugged. "I only said they were going to be grandparents. I didn't tell them to come."

"But you didn't dissuade them either." Misty gave an irritated shake of her head, but he just grinned, unrepentant, and followed her to the door.

"Darling!" Althea Harrison burst into the foyer. "A baby! It's so exciting." She hugged Misty and then her son.

"Congratulations, my dear," Luc's father said more quietly but no less happily, if the light in his eyes was any indication.

Althea sailed into the living room, the others following in her wake. "I called everyone, and, of course, they're all delighted. Alice insists that we make a formal announcement at a special little party."

"There's no need," Luc said, his laughing glance going to Misty, who was staring in amazement in response to Althea's suggestion.

"But we must do something," Luc's mother wailed.

"We could put it in the morning's listings on the stock exchange. They go worldwide," James Harrison suggested.

"Could we do that?" His wife's eyes glittered.

"No, of course not. Dad's teasing you." Luc laughed at his mother's crestfallen expression.

"Well, I'll think of something," she declared.

"No doubt," her husband murmured, winking at Misty.

"Now, dear, tell me how you're feeling. Who's your doctor? Will you go to a hospital or have the baby at home? Are you going to continue to work?"

The last question brought Luc's head up. He stared at his wife, waiting for her answer.

"I think I'll work for a little while longer," she said hesitantly.

"All right, darling," he agreed, "but I reserve the right to take you off the job if I think you're getting too tired."

"Luc, I'll be fine." She smiled at him, feeling even more relaxed in response to his concern. She turned to her in-laws. "You will stay the night, won't you? It would worry me to have you travel back to the Island so late at night."

Althea glanced at her husband, who nodded, "Of course, we will, dear. It's so kind of you to offer."

"That will be great, Dad," Luc interjected. "You can come to the office tomorrow. You said you wanted to take a look at the Gennser plan."

"Good idea." James grinned at Misty.

Althea rolled her eyes. "I should have known he would insist on going to that foolish bank."

"I could go to that foolish bank every day if I wanted to, my dear. Have you forgotten that there are branches all over New York State, including several near us?"

"Yes, but it's always been the main branch that drew you. 'That's where all the action is,' you used to say."

"Ummm. Did I say that?" he mused, grinning.

Misty was delighted to watch Luc's parents interact.

When his mother described Luc as a boy, she had to laugh. "My dear, he was the original *enfant terrible*. He took a frog to dancing class, and seven mothers called me to complain. Oh yes, you laugh now, but you'll have to be on your guard with your own child. Those same awful genes may be passed on," she pronounced in mock funereal tones.

For Misty, Althea's teasing revived very serious fears. What if she *did* pass on bad genes to her child? She caught Luc watching her and gave him a shaky smile.

He relaxed visibly. "I like to see you smile."

James Harrison set his brandy glass down on an inlaid rosewood table next to his chair. His shrewd gaze remained on Luc for long moments before going to Misty.

Luc grinned at his father. "She's beautiful, isn't she?"

"Yes," James Harrison agreed, nodding solemnly.

"Stop it, both of you," Althea said tartly. "You're making Mystique blush."

Luc rose from his seat and pulled Misty to her feet, wrapping an arm around her. He sank back into his wide chair and pulled her onto his lap. "Is my darling blushing?" he asked softly.

"Luc, for heaven's sake." Misty pushed against his chest with one hand, trying to keep her blouse from riding up with the other.

James laughed. "Relax, my dear. A man always likes to hold the woman he loves. Occasionally I still chase Althea around the house."

"It's true," Luc's mother admitted readily. "But we never cavort in front of the hired help," she added sternly. She beamed at Misty. "Don't worry, my dear. You only have day help."

"See?" Luc said in dulcet tones, his eyes alight with amusement as he looked down at her spread across his lap.

Helpless laughter assailed Misty as she clung to him, taking in the indulgent glances of her in-laws. "You shouldn't encourage him," she told Althea.

"Too true. The Harrison men need very little encouragement to be arrogant." Althea lifted a stubborn chin and nodded insistently when the men protested.

"And no crowing from you, mama-to-be." Luc kissed Misty's hair and held her closer.

The evening was one of the happiest and most carefree Misty could remember.

That night after she and Luc had gone to their room, she undressed while Luc did some paperwork in his study. Wrapped in a silk robe, she peeked in to see how he was doing and decided not to disturb him, since he seemed to be completely absorbed.

Feeling restless, she went down to the kitchen to get a bottle of mineral water from the refrigerator. But when she opened the kitchen door, she saw that the light was on.

"Come in and shut the door," Luc's father greeted her. He was wearing Luc's maroon robe, and his hair was still damp from a shower. "Althea's asleep, or I wouldn't be down here. She's trying to break me of my nocturnal eating habits." He chuckled and, sticking his head inside the refrigerator, brought out two plastic-wrapped packages. "Turkey, chicken, or ham?" he offered.

Misty chuckled. "Actually, I'd rather have some mineral water and unsalted crackers."

James nodded. "Ah, yes. Easier on the digestion."

"But I've always enjoyed raiding the refrigerator." She refrained from telling him that scrounging for food at night when her parents were sound asleep had been the only way to avoid the constant carping that had become habitual during mealtimes in the Carver home.

"Good." James Harrison paused, then grimaced. "My dear, forgive me. I've been rude. This is your home, and I've encroached. My children are used to my eccentricities, but you—"

"I want you to feel completely at home," she assured him, taking the meat packages from his hands, then retrieving pickles and other condiments from the refrigerator.

James kissed her cheek and gently pushed her into a chair. "I'll be the waiter."

When they settled down at last, they had a table full of food from which to choose, plus milk and mineral water to drink.

"Mystique," James began, swallowing a bite of a chicken sandwich, "I have never seen my son so relaxed and carefree. I noticed in the last few years that he'd become colder and more cynical. I didn't think he would ever find the happiness he's found with you." He patted her hand.

Misty flushed with pleasure. "I didn't think we would be so happy, either." She shrugged. "We seemed poles apart at first."

She and her father-in-law chatted easily on a variety of subjects. Misty was pleased to have this chance to get to know James better. In some ways he was so like Luc; in other ways he was very different. Comparing the two men fascinated her.

They had just finished eating when a voice said from the doorway, "So here you are." Luc was standing there, glaring at his father. Now what was wrong? Misty wondered.

James chuckled. "Feathers ruffled?"

"A little," Luc admitted, going behind Misty's chair and leaning over her. "I didn't know you were hungry, darling."

"Want a cracker?" she asked.

He took the cracker she offered him, then pulled a chair up close to hers.

"I thought your wife might enjoy a little intelligent conversation," James told his son. "I don't imagine she gets much, living with you."

Misty laughed and Luc glowered as his father rose from the table and leaned over to kiss her on top of the head. "My dear, we will do this again. I enjoyed it."

"Don't count on it," Luc retorted.

"Thank you," Misty said simultaneously.

"Good night." James was chuckling softly as he left the kitchen.

Sudden silence filled the room. Misty couldn't control the giggle that escaped her. Luc stared at her, then lifted her hand to nibble on her pinky finger. "All right, so I was jealous."

Stunned, Misty stared at him. "You were not!"

He moved his mouth to her next finger and nodded without looking up. "Yes, I was. Why do you think Dad was enjoying himself so much? He knew."

"Luc." Misty was confused.

"It's stupid, I know, but I didn't want him feeding you down here. I wanted to do it."

As Misty stared at his scowling face, a surge of love swept over her. "Your father was already here when I arrived," she explained. "I came for some mineral water and crackers." She leaned forward and kissed him on the nose.

Before she could pull back, he slid his mouth over hers. "Do you want more crackers?" he whispered.

"No," she whispered back.

"Good." He stood up and pulled her from her chair. "Shall I bring the mineral water upstairs?"

"Not unless you want some," Misty murmured, leaning against him.

"No, I'm fine. But the next time you want something, tell me and I'll get it for you," he insisted, a mulish look returning to his face.

"That's fine with me." Misty felt kitten-comfortable cuddled to his chest, yet she was tingling with excitement because she knew Luc was going to make love to her when they returned to their room.

CHAPTER TEN

It was the evening before the event that Luc, his father, and his brothers-in-law had begun calling "the Stampede," the coming-out party for Misty's sisters. Misty had been deliriously happy all day. She and Luc had met with Dr. Mellon for two hours, and she'd begun to hope that her fears regarding motherhood might someday be put to rest. She intended to continue to meet with the doctor at least once a month during her pregnancy.

She'd been flattered and surprised by the reactions of Luc's family to her pregnancy. Alice had insisted on planning a baby shower to be held at the family's Long Island country club.

"With three hundred guests, you can be sure," Ted had whispered to her.

Her sisters had been thrilled to learn about the baby. They had come to New York to visit and dragged her to F.A.O. Schwarz, where they'd tried to talk her into buying a six-foot-tall stuffed bear. She'd laughed and shaken her head.

"I suppose Misty is right," Celia had finally conceded. "It might scare the baby."

For some time now Mrs. Wheaton had been preparing meals according to the diet Luc and Dr. Wagner had worked out together, despite Misty's protests.

Dr. Wagner had taken Misty aside. "Indulge him on this, Misty. He's so worried about you."

"But I'm as normal as can be."

"I know, but he's so used to being in control, and having this baby is one thing he *can't* control. He needs to feel he's taking part somehow."

"Not Luc!" Misty was incredulous.

"Oh, yes, Luc," Dr. Wagner had insisted, laughing.

Now, as Misty packed their clothes for a weekend on Long Island with his family, she smiled to herself.

"You'd better be thinking about me," Luc murmured directly behind her, making her jump. He slipped his arms around her waist and pulled her back against him. "That dreamy expression had better be for me."

"It is. But I didn't expect you home for another two hours."

"I know. But I started to miss you and decided to come home and help you pack."

Misty turned in his arms and lifted a hand to his cheek. "We're only going for the weekend. There isn't much to pack."

His arms closed around her. "You aren't supposed to do any lifting. Yesterday Mrs. Wheaton said she found you cleaning the bathroom."

"Luc, I was only wiping around the tub after my shower."

"That's what we hire people to do. A cleaning woman comes in three days a week."

Misty stared up at his truculent expression and laughed. "I love your little-boy look."

He leaned closer, his nose rubbing hers. "I like hearing you say things like that." He stared at her for a moment, his eyes going over her face and hair before returning to her mouth. "I don't suppose you love the little boy behind the little-boy look."

"I don't love the little boy," Misty agreed, seeing a flicker of emotion in his eyes, "but I do love the man." She finished

in a barely audible voice, feeling as if the few remaining
barriers between them had abruptly fallen away.

Luc's arms fell to his sides, and a muscle in his mouth
twitched.

"Luc," Misty whispered, feeling the blood drain from
her face. He must be angry with her for saying those words,
for threatening to destroy the casual rapport they shared by
declaring her love.

But to her relief he touched her chin with one finger and
said, "And will you stay with me always?"

"You told me only ninety years," she said.

"Now I want ninety-five."

"Is this a bargain?"

"Yes. I love you, Mystique Harrison, and I never thought
it would mean so much to hear you say you love me. You
did say that, didn't you?"

"I did."

"Angel . . ." His voice broke. "Would you like to renew
our vows in a church?"

Misty blinked. "Oh! I never thought . . . Well, yes, I
would."

"Good. I want to be married five times—in three
churches, one chapel, and a garden," Luc said lazily, not
taking his eyes from her face.

Misty felt the power of his passion like a physical force
that threatened to overwhelm her. "Luc, sometimes I'm
frightened by the intensity of our feeling for one another."

"But you trust me, don't you, darling?"

"In every possible way."

The brilliance of his smile dazzled her. "We're getting
there, aren't we, love?" he said. "Step by step, word by
word?"

She nodded, too filled with emotion to speak. Feeling
suddenly shy, she sought to direct the conversation to a
lighter subject. "Do you think my sisters will have a good
time tonight?"

He let his hands fall to her waist but didn't pull her
closer. "Yes, I think the girls will have a good time. My
sisters will have invited every eligible young man of a suit-
able age in the whole county for them."

"Ummm. No one ever did that for me," she quipped,

glancing flirtatiously up at him. It surprised her to see irritation cross his face. "Can't you take a joke?" she chided.

"Not about you, I can't."

"Silly." She stretched up to kiss his chin.

Being sure of his love gave her such confidence. She
felt completely at ease with him. And all of a sudden she
wanted to tell him everything about her past. They would
have no secrets from each other ever again—nothing but
complete honesty from this day forward.

"Luc," she began, "you once told me you didn't want to
know anything about Richard and Leonard, but I want to
tell you about them now. I don't want to hurt you, but I do
want to settle once and for all any doubts you might have
about me because of them."

Luc's expression was unreadable. "I don't have any doubts
about you."

"Please, Luc. It would make me feel better."

He regarded her uncertainly. "All right," he said at last.
"Tell me."

She gathered her thoughts. "I want you to understand
that I didn't get involved with them out of love. I didn't
know what love was. I thought it was an illusion, a fancy
name for need, desire, lust. When I got involved with first
Richard and later Leonard, I just wanted to be happy. I
knew I didn't love them, and I didn't think they loved me.
I neither wanted nor expected such an emotion." She lifted
a palm to either side of Luc's face and didn't flinch at his
intense gaze. "Sex with them meant nothing to me. It wasn't
even very pleasurable."

Luc's taut muscles seemed to relax. "It wasn't?"

Misty shook her head and smiled. "If you want to know
the truth, I felt more sensually aware while taking a hot
mineral bath than I did when I was in bed with either man."

Luc chuckled. They grinned at each other in a silent
sharing of intimate secrets.

"I didn't know anyone like you existed," Misty resumed.
"Until you started making such a pest of yourself at the
Terrace Hotel. Thank goodness you're a persistent man,
Luc Harrison." She grew more serious. "At first I thought
that what I felt for you must be an illusion. But it grew
stronger and stronger every day, blowing apart all my pre-

conceived notions about commitments and relationships."
She laughed. "I have to admit that, in the beginning, I
expected you at any moment to turn from Dr. Jekyll into
Mr. Hyde."

"I noticed," he murmured.

"I didn't want to love you."

"I know."

"But you wouldn't leave me alone."

"I was fighting for my life," he said, massaging her waist
with strong fingers.

"Am I your life?"

"Yes."

"But how can you love me?" As soon as the words fell
from her mouth, she bit her lips. "I didn't mean to sound
self-deprecating, but all the newspapers in New York said
you would marry someone from your own social set. That
made sense to me." She clutched his shoulders. "Even though,
now that I have you, I won't let you go."

"Feel free to chain me to you, love," Luc murmured
against her cheek. "And as for my set, as you call it, you
are my set. You fit in perfectly with my family, and they
all love you."

"They do?" Misty felt herself swell with pleasure. "Oh,
Luc, I'm getting so conceited being married to you."

"Not true. You've just gained a sense of your own worth.
You're beginning to realize how much you mean to me,
how important you are. That realization has given you confidence."

She rubbed her cheek against his shirt. "I do feel better
about myself."

"Good. And are you beginning to believe that you and
I will make good parents?"

She nodded slowly. "I suppose I'll always have some
doubts."

"No, you won't, darling. After a time you'll begin to
know what I know already—that you'll be a fine mother."

Together they finished packing, teasing and laughing,
pausing frequently to share quick kisses and brief caresses.
Finally they left for Long Island, wrapped in their own
special aura of love.

The next day was a hectic one for the Harrison family. Luc's sister Velma and her husband Ken arrived, and Misty was able to renew her acquaintance with their daughter Janie, who chatted excitedly at Misty's side.

"My mother said Mark and Mary are coming with their parents and some of your other friends will be coming."

"Yes. Morey and Zena will be here, too, and—"

"I can't wait," Janie cried, clapping her hands. Then she covered her mouth. "I didn't mean to interrupt, Aunt Mystique."

"You didn't." Misty put her arm around the girl, delighted at being called Aunt Mystique. "Shall we go get Jennifer and take her for a walk?"

"Yes!" Then Janie looked around her and whispered, "But we'll have to take James and Gregory, too."

Misty nodded.

"Well, Aunt Mystique, we better watch out. The last time I took the boys for a walk, they jumped into the fish pond, and I ruined my best jeans getting them out."

Misty laughed. "Well, we'll have to keep a sharp eye on them, then. It's way too early to go swimming in Long Island."

Misty and Janie were both kept busy entertaining the boys as they pushed Jennifer in the English buggy provided by the housekeeper.

"I wish Uncle Luc didn't have to go with Grandpa and Daddy to help at the club," Janie said wistfully. "Then they could have walked with us. James and Greg would have behaved better." She ran off to retrieve the two boys from a thicket of bushes at the end of the curving driveway.

As they retraced their steps, Misty heard a car behind them and quickly ushered the boys, Janie, and the buggy to the side of the road. "Janie!" Mary shouted from the car window as she sped past with the rest of her family and Morey and Zena.

Misty and her troupe hurried back to the house, where they were greeted by a flurry of activity. Everyone was talking and laughing, making the old structure seem to echo with happy sounds and good feelings.

Since the very young children would not be accompanying the adults to the dinner dance that evening, they were indulged with an early dinner party of their own. Misty played the piano and sang "The Rainbow Connection," which the Muppets had made famous. The children crowded around her and sang boisterously.

"I think my wife is enjoying herself," Luc said, coming up behind her.

Misty laughed, a little out of breath. "I'm having a great time. Come and sing along with us."

Without further urging, Luc joined in, his lusty baritone standing out among the children's high voices and Misty's clear mezzo-soprano.

When it was time to go, Misty regretted having to leave the youngsters with the housekeeper. "Any fool can see that you love children, darling," Luc said as they left the room and climbed the stairs to their suite. "Soon you'll be able to see that for yourself."

"I think so," Misty said, squeezing his hand. "I think so."

Half an hour later they were on their way to the country club, where Luc's family had been members for generations. As soon as she stepped into the foyer, Misty could tell that the evening would be an unqualified success. The rooms were already crowded with beautifully dressed guests, and she was immediately caught up in the glamour and excitement. Alice was beaming, and Althea's cheeks glowed pink with the warmth of good feeling.

After chatting over cocktails, everyone sat down to a sumptuous dinner. Misty could only taste a bit of each of the many dishes. Afterward, she was standing with Morey, Zena, David, and Aileen when her mother-in-law sailed up to the group, her eyes sparkling. "Morey, I must take you with me." She turned to Misty. "Wanda Gump is green with envy over the girls' dresses. She insisted on meeting Morey, but I told her he's so exclusive that he'd have to interview her before taking her on as a customer." Althea grinned impishly, Misty laughed, and Morey went limp with nervousness. "Don't worry, dear, Alice and I will carry the ball," Althea assured him. She left with Morey in tow.

Zena and Aileen laughed out loud. "Morey will be as limp as a rag when we see him next," Zena predicted.

"A rich rag if Mrs. Harrison has her say," David mused,

smiling at Misty. "She's quite a woman."

"She's absolutely wonderful," Misty agreed.

"And I've never seen you looking better, Misty," David added.

"You do look wonderful, Mist," Aileen concurred.

"Thank you. If I do, it's because I'm happy," she answered, knowing that she could never begin to describe what she and Luc shared. How could she convey the delirious feeling of freedom that love had given her? What words could she use to draw a picture of the sweet ecstasy that was theirs alone?

Luc had led off the dancing by escorting Celia onto the floor while John danced with Marcy and Ted danced with Betsy. Now, as the three young women continued to dance with fresh-faced college men, Luc came up to Misty and asked, "May I borrow my wife for this dance?"

Misty slipped eagerly into his arms, and they whirled onto the crowded floor. "I thought I was never going to be able to dance with you," Luc complained, holding her close.

"You looked very good out there with my sisters," Misty said.

"And you look gorgeous in that sea-green silk dress. But I can see your legs through that slit every time you move, Mrs. Harrison." He shook his head in mock reproof, making her laugh. "It's not funny," he chided.

She lifted both hands and locked them behind his neck. "I love it when you act possessive, Mr. Harrison."

"Watch it, lady. See what I mean?" He pressed intimately against her.

"Darling, you're aroused! Shall we excuse ourselves?" Misty teased.

"Damn. If we only could," Luc muttered, glancing around.

"I was only teasing, Luc," Misty protested, laughing. "We can't leave, so take that mulish look off your face."

When the dance ended, they found themselves standing next to Betsy, who turned to introduce them to her escort.

"Luc, Misty, this is Kevin Short. Kevin, this is my sister, Misty Harrison, and my brother-in-law, Luc Harrison." Betsy's eyes shone with delight. "Kevin is in my Irish literature class."

Kevin smiled. "Hello."

"Misty is going to have a baby," Betsy announced proudly. Although Misty's cheeks flamed with embarrassment at the announcement, and Luc gave a muffled chuckle, Kevin remained coolly poised.

"I know, your Aunt Alice already told me, as did your grandmother. Your family seems to be pretty excited about the news."

"Yes," Misty said shyly. She glared at Luc, who laughed out loud.

"Sorry, darling. I guess I'm excited about the baby, too," he explained.

Kevin's puzzled look cleared. "Yeah." Then he glanced at Betsy and the couples gyrating on the floor to a fast rock beat. "Want to try it again?" he asked.

Betsy grinned. "Excuse us, please."

Misty took Luc's hand and pulled him into the surging crowd, too. "Are you sure it's okay for you to do this?" He frowned down at her as they moved to the wild rhythms.

"Absolutely. And stop treating me as if I were going to give birth to the first two-headed donkey."

Luc laughed. "I know I'm being difficult, but you'll just have to bear with me, darling."

Misty was about to answer when Ted and Deirdre swept up to them. "Misty, if it's a boy, you could name him after me—Edward. That's a great name."

"Don't be silly," Deirdre admonished. "She won't know the sex of the child for months yet. But you know, Edward isn't a bad name. If it's a girl, you can call her Edwina."

"Good Lord!" Luc exclaimed.

"I had an Aunt Edwina," Ted said defensively. A reluctant grin spread across his face. "Of course she weighed one hundred and eighty pounds and was five feet three inches."

"True." Deirdre sighed. "Do you think you'll choose one of the family names, Mystique?"

"We haven't even had a chance to think about it yet," she said.

"Family names," Luc mused, his arm still around Misty. "Didn't Mother have a cousin Eufemia?"

Deirdre closed her eyes. "Don't start."

"And she had a brother Eustace," Ted added with relish.

Misty began shaking her head, looking from one to the other.

"And wasn't there one named Tadpole?" Ted asked.

Misty gasped.

"That was Claypool," Deirdre corrected tartly as her husband burst into laughter. "That's the southern branch of mother's family—the Carters," she explained to Misty.

"Oh."

"I forgot to mention Cousin Lipscomb," Luc continued. "We called him Lippy."

"That can't be true!" Misty exclaimed.

"Of course it's true," Ted said, looking hurt. "Cousin Lipscomb was one of the most renowned icthyologists in all of Nevada."

"An icthyologist? In Nevada?" Misty said faintly.

Deirdre shrugged, sidestepping an energetic dancer who had come too close. "Strange, isn't it? He *was* eccentric."

"And subject to seasickness," Luc finished.

Misty looked blank as Ted chuckled and Deirdre smiled.

"Hadn't we better dance or something?" Misty suggested.

"I'd rather eat," Ted said, distastefully eyeing the jouncing couples on the floor.

"Would you like something to eat, darling?" Luc glanced down at her, his eyes alight.

"I'm not hungry, but I *would* like something to drink." As Misty took his arm, she noted that several women were assessing her husband from the dance floor. They passed into a smaller room with a round table set with assortments of canapés. "I can't believe anyone could want more food after the dinner we just ate."

"I heard that," Ted said, spearing a shrimp. "I'll have you know, sister-in-law, that I need continual sustenance when dealing with the Harrison clan."

"Amen to that," Luc murmured.

"Do you really have a cousin named Lipscomb?" Misty asked Luc when Ted and Deirdre had turned away to speak to someone else. "Or were you just trying to make me laugh?"

Luc paused, a glass of Irish whisky and water poised at

his lips, his eyes sparkling with amusement. "You know me too well, dear wife."

"And I like what I know." Her eyes widened, and she watched fascinated as Luc's face flushed with embarrassment.

He leaned closer and whispered, "Tell me that tonight, will you, when I'm holding you in my arms and your bare skin is rubbing against mine."

"Luc!" Misty gasped and looked around to see if anyone had heard. "Stop that."

"Too late. The image of you naked on our bed is implanted in my brain." He tipped the rest of his drink into his mouth and set down the glass. "Enough of that."

"But, Luc, you haven't had much of anything to drink. Just a few champagne toasts and this glass of whisky."

He grinned at her. "Checking up on me? But you're right, I haven't had much to drink. I find I don't want much when I'm with you. I want nothing that will cloud my thinking or blunt my awareness. You're all the stimulation I need. In fact, sometimes you're too much stimulation."

"Oh, dear, I do hate to interrupt you, but I was wondering, Mystique dear, would you play for us?"

Startled out of their tête-à-tête, Misty and Luc turned to see Althea. "Mother," Luc warned, obviously not approving of her suggestion.

"I know, I know. You don't want any of us to bother Mystique in any way. You made that very clear. But, Luc, surely it isn't a bother to ask her to play for us."

"Of course I'll play for you, Mother," Misty agreed.

Luc's mother beamed. "Did you hear that, Luc? She called me Mother." She stretched up and kissed Misty on the cheek. "We all love you, dear, and you needn't play if you don't want to. You're such a beautiful woman. I just know your babies will be beautiful, too."

"See?" Luc led Misty across the massive solarium and into a front room, where a piano stood on a small platform. "I'm not the only one who knows what a wonderful mother you'll make."

"Oh, Luc," Misty said, her eyes filling with tears.

"Don't cry," he whispered, "or I'll have to carry you out

of here and up the stairs to make love to you."

She gave him a watery smile. "Oh, Luc, Luc, I love you so..."

Misty's mother-in-law had just finished quieting the guests, and Misty began to play, her eyes rarely leaving Luc's face. Afterward, her enraptured audience burst into enthusiastic applause.

As Misty rose from the piano bench and accepted Luc's kiss, she felt that her world was complete. She had Luc, a loving family, and, coming soon, a baby she would love with all her heart. She'd come so far in such a short time— and all because of Luc's fierce and unwavering love. "I adore you," she whispered, the words coming easily to her now.

With a brilliant smile, amid the compliments and congratulations of the guests, Luc led Misty out of the room and home to their bedroom, where they made love far into the night.

Two years later, Misty and Luc went on a skiing trip to Sweetgum Lodge. As they removed their heavy clothing after spending a morning on the slopes, Misty turned to find her husband's eyes on her. "What is it, darling?"

"I can't believe we've had two children only ten months apart. Ten months!" Luc shook his head. "You leave me reeling. My mother and father are still bragging to all their friends, and your husband is at your feet."

"Never," Misty exclaimed in mock disbelief, happiness welling up inside her. "You don't regret having Mary Deirdre so soon after Stuy, do you?" she asked.

"I regret nothing, my lovely wife, except that I wish we had more time alone." He grimaced when she chuckled. "Even though I work at home two days a week, I still don't have as much time with you as I'd like."

"You'll get tired of me," Misty predicted, teasing him. She had perfect confidence in Luc's loyalty to her. He had made her whole. She knew that she was a good mother and, although Lucas Stuyvesant Harrison II was a little devil who kept his mother and his nurse chasing after him every waking moment, Misty was confident in her dealings with both children.

"How is it that your waist is still so tiny after having had two babies? Your legs are so slender, so long." Luc tossed his ski vest toward a corner of the room. The thermal shirt he was wearing emphasized his muscled chest. "You're still the sexiest woman in the world."

"I always want to look attractive to you. That's a thrill for me," she said softly.

Luc stopped cold and stared at her. "I'm five feet away from you, yet I feel as if we're making love. I'm most alive when I'm in your arms, my sweet. Your very special loving aura surrounds me," he whispered. "I'm constantly captivated by the mystique of your personality. That's the main reason I continued to call you Mystique even after you told me your name was Misty." His voice dropped lower. "From the first moment I saw you that night in the Edwardian Room of the Terrace Hotel, I was drawn to you, and I've never wanted to leave you since then. At first, I thought it would be great to have you as a lover. Then I imagined the moment when I would have to leave you, and I realized I could *never* leave you." He took a step closer. "That realization had the impact of a bomb dropped on my life." He smiled. "You're my Mystique, and I belong to you. No matter how many wonderful children we have, no matter what challenges we face, that will never change."

"I know, Luc. And I love you."

Misty smiled serenely as she glided into his arms.

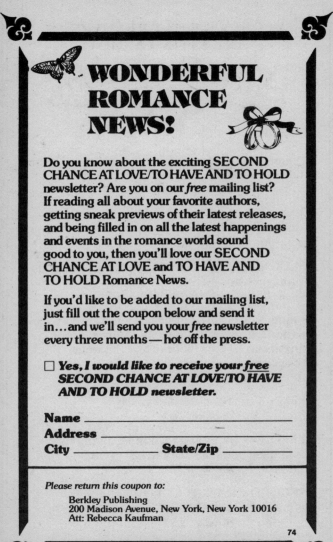

HERE'S WHAT READERS ARE SAYING ABOUT

Second Chance at Love

"I think your books are great. I love to read them, as does my family."
— P. C., Milford, MA*

"Your books are some of the best romances I've read."
— M. B., Zeeland, MI*

"SECOND CHANCE AT LOVE is my favorite line of romance novels."
— L. B., Springfield, VA*

"I think SECOND CHANCE AT LOVE books are terrific. I married my 'Second Chance' over 15 years ago. I truly believe love is lovelier the second time around!"
— P. P., Houston, TX*

"I enjoy your books tremendously."
— I. S., Bayonne, NJ*

"I love your books and read them all the time. Keep them coming—they're just great."
— G. L., Brookfield, CT*

"SECOND CHANCE AT LOVE books are definitely the best!"
— D. P., Wabash, IN*

*Name and address available upon request

Second Chance at Love®

All of the above titles are $1.95
Prices may be slightly higher in Canada.
